I'll See You in the Morning

Joanne C. Jensen

PublishAmerica
Baltimore

First printing

ISBN: 1–59129–422–3
PUBLISHED BY PUBLISH AMERICA
BOOK PUBLISHERS
www.publishamerica.com
Baltimore

Printed in the United States of America

Dedication

Jon Derek, this book is dedicated to you, son, your joy for life still fills my heart with laughter and your final words to me, "I'll see you in the morning," fills my heart with joy and hope for the future.

Dear Jenifer
Thank you for your
kindness toward John & I —
Forever Grateful
Joanne C. Jensen

Acknowledgment

To my husband John, who has used his abilities as a teacher to edit and type the original manuscript; to my daughter Holly, who took time from her own work in graphic arts to design the cover of this book; to my daughter Melodie, who has whisked me away many times to new adventures, giving me new insight into my writings; and to the memory of my precious son, Jon Derek, who has gone home to be with the Lord. The incredible joy he put into each moment of his, and other's, life is an inspiration to me, and helps me to continue with my writings.

Chapter One

"The humidity was exasperating and Jenny's scurrying around didn't lessen its intensity. She dabbed at her moist face with the corner of her long coarse apron. The muggy air seemed to suck the breath forcibly from her being.

"Why, oh, why?" she muttered to herself as she poured water from the kettle to wash the supper dishes.

"Why did I ever allow Jacque to bring us to this... this desolate and forsaken farm," she continued as she peered thoughtfully through the cracked and weather beaten windows at the muddy, swollen river.

Summers deplorable weather only increased their miserable living conditions. Constant rains washed out the little garden Jenny and the children had worked so hard to plant. The river had nearly doubled in width and was spilling muddy water all along the bottom land. Instead of giving any kind of cool relief, the rain only intensified the sweltering Kansas heat.

The farm consisted of forty acres, a little over twenty on rich flat bottom land along the meandering Missouri River. The remainder was pasture land on high ground, too hilly and full of rocks to grow much of anything but forage for the stock.

In the months since Jacque had brought them here, he had made no attempt to farm the land, nor did he appear to have any intentions of doing so in the future. This was a source of great contention for Jenny and to add to it all she was greatly mystified by Jacque and his friends puzzling activities.

"Oh, mercy," declared Jenny, "the water pail is empty again."

"I'll have to go to the spring before nightfall," she thought to herself as she pushed back a strand of auburn hair that had tumbled down over her forehead.

"What's the use," she lamented, staring at herself in the cracked mirror above the washbasin. Hard work and grief had taken their toll and she felt old far beyond her tender age of twenty–three.

She took the pail from the stand and started for the ridge above and behind the house. The spring up near the barn was their only source of fresh cold water.

"Looks like more rain," she sighed in discouragement as she started up the sloping incline.

The constant drone and intermittent humming of insects on the ridge beyond became incessantly noisy with the setting of the sun. It pulsated in her ears until at times it was unbearable.

She was thankful that Robbie and Elizabeth along with baby Jacqueline had fallen asleep soon after the evening chores were done. Jenny had saved enough supper for Jacque in case he was to return tonight, but his comings and goings were so irrational that it was hard to tell when he would arrive.

The ground sloshed wet under her high–topped shoes as she made her way across the soggy ground. Dark clouds hung low above the bluff and lightning flashed and thundered as tiny fingers of light splintered across the distant sky.

Jenny had only taken a few steps up the hill when she became aware of someone coming down the slope toward her.

Her slender hand trembled on the handle of the pail.

"It must be Jacque," she anguished, as she unconsciously belt the bruises on her face from his farewell a few days ago.

No, it wasn't him, Jenny concluded with a sigh of relief. She stared intently into the gathering dusk of evening, in the direction of the oncoming figure, her heart still beating hard.

"Mrs. Boshart," called the husky voice of a man as he came nearer. "It's me, Mr. Schultz! I do not wish to frighten you," he was quick to explain, "but I have a letter for you," all the while waving the letter above his head as if to convince her.

"The letter carrier asked me if I would mind delivering this to you. So many of the roads are washed out he wasn't sure he could get through to you or not," he added.

"I didn't realize it was you, Mr. Schultz, until you came closer," declared Jenny with a sigh of relief.

"Thank you," she said as he placed the envelope into her outstretched hand, still trembling partly because of the shock it might be Jacque, and partly because she was excited about receiving her first letter since Jacque brought her to this forsaken place.

Mr. Schultz was well aware of the jeopardy in which he placed his life, simply by stepping foot on Jacque's property. An attempted social call from the good man and his wife several months ago had ended in near tragedy when Jacque had run them off at the end of a gun.

Jenny whirled around in the direction of the house wondering who would be sending here a letter? Her feet felt like lead in the soggy shoes slowing her down and making the journey to the house seem like miles. Soon she managed to reach the doorway breathing heavily in short gasps.

Pushing herself through the doorway, she hurried to light a lamp as the room was now almost enveloped in darkness. A scan of the envelope revealed its' postmark was from St. Louis. She made haste to rip open the letter, all the while looking and listening, fearful that Jacque would soon appear. The letter read:

Barton and Barton Attorneys at Law
St. Louis, Missouri
July 21, 1908

Dear Mrs. Boshart:

Difficulty in obtaining a proper mailing address had caused us great delay in reaching you. We were finally able to secure such after we received a recent letter written by your husband, a Mr. Jacque Boshart, requesting information concerning your deceased husbands' life insurance policy.

Let us assure you that we have done everything possible to process your claim. However, it will be necessary for you to personally come to our office in St. Louis, as your signature is needed on the final documents. Your claim will be settled forthwith.

We would be most appreciative if you would comply within the week or as soon as possible. Our location is on the second floor of the St. Louis Bank and Trust Building. We trust that our delay in finding you has caused you no hardship.

We offer our sincere regrets at your former husbands' passing. He was highly respected, a fine Christian man and always conscientious in all his business dealings.

Respectfully yours,
Joseph J. Barton
Attorney at Law

"Jacque must not see this letter," Jenny stammered to herself after reading its contents.

Frantically she looked about the room for a hiding place. Where could she put it where it would be safe form Jacque's prying eyes? Perhaps behind the cupboard she reasoned as she reached behind the cabinet that held her few dishes and meager food supplies. She felt for a crack between the logs, finding one she slipped the letter carefully between the logs, hoping it would remain hidden secure and out of sight.

Until now, Jenny wasn't even aware that David had a life insurance policy, but apparently, Jacque did. Then she gasped at the sudden thought that Jacque rushed her into this marriage for the insurance money. He had already taken what little David had left her and the children.

It was only recently that Jenny became sure that Jacque had believed she was keeping some dark secret from him. Jacque had questioned her incessantly about David's business and even about her own childhood, of which there was little to tell. It was common knowledge that Jenny's mother worked in a tavern...that was no secret. At fourteen Jenny had married David who at Twenty–four had already established the hardware store left to him by his father. Blissfully, they had lived in some of the rooms behind the store and Jenny had found happiness like she never knew before. She found love for the first time, turning her lonely existence into a life of great joy and fulfillment as in quick succession, Robbie, Elizabeth, and Jacqueline came to share their happiness.

It was a few months before David's untimely accident that Jacque had shown up. It seemed he was a younger brother of David's mother. He stated that he would like to make a small investment in the store so David took him into the business and soon he became a full partner.

Jacque was caring and attentive after David's death and Jenny who had collapsed into a state of shock and grief, fell easy prey to Jacque's pretentious concern for her and the children's well being. In the throes of her deep depression she had allowed Jacque to manipulate her into a quick marriage...even yet to this day she could not clearly remember the details of that day.

So bewildered by the turn of events, she was not aware that Jacque without her permission had sold the business and later claimed they needed the money to pay back bills.

The handsome, charming, and soft–spoken Jacque now became a violent and cruel person, especially towards her and the children. They were terrified of him and his frequent rages. He took up with unscrupulous characters who he brought consistently into the house, in spite of her objections.

Directly after the sale of the business, Jacque made a sudden decision to move from St. Louis, Missouri to this desolate farm just outside of Kansas City, Kansas. He simply announced one morning that the house and hardware store were sold and that they were moving. Within the week they were packed and on a train to Kansas. They took only what they could carry and pack as baggage. Jacque put them on the train and immediately left on one of his mysterious trips explaining that one of his associates would meet them at the station to take them to the farm.

After a long journey filled with dread and uncertainty, they finally arrived at their destination. After an hour of anxiously awaiting for an unknown associate a rude unsociable character appeared and after taking their bags motioned for them to get into the wagon where he had previously thrown their baggage. With fearful apprehension and anxiety, Jenny lifted the children one by one into the dirty dusty wagon. With a crack of the whip and simultaneous cursing, they were off at a frenzied gallop. Holding on for dear life Jenny repeatedly pleaded for the man to slow down, but to no avail. About half-way from the station to the farm, a wheel came off, making it necessary for them to stop. The driver became enraged, cussing and kicking the wheel and then sitting down on a rock he pulled out a bottle from his coat pocket and guzzled down its contents. Then after a few impolite grunts, he staggered back into the direction from which they came. Jenny and the children were stranded and alone. It was sometime later that Mr. Schultz and his wife came upon the scene. They graciously offered to help. When Jenny gave them the location of the farm to the best of her recollection, Mrs. Schultz said that they were going right by the place on the way home and would be more than happy to escort them to the farm. Jenny remembered how stunned Mr. Schultz had been at the discovery that the farm had been sold. He didn't think old Gus would ever sell that place.

A sudden noise somewhere in the distance along the ridge roused Jenny from her thoughts. Was it a gunshot? Jenny hoped not. Perhaps it was a clap of thunder.

Oh, no! The water, she suddenly remembered as she surveyed the bottom of the empty container. She had forgotten to fill the water pail. She grasped the handle but before she reached the door the unmistakable sound of horses hooves could be heard thundering along the upper ridge. Her heart beat wildly. Her cheeks flushed crimson against her pail complexion. She prayed Jacque had not come upon Mr. Schultz on the ridge above. There was no time to bring water from the spring. Besides, she had no desire to meet up with Jacque and his rough companions on the path. She placed the empty pail back in its place on the stand just as Jacque came thundering into the room followed by his noisy companions.

"Well, aren't you a sight," he sneered as Jenny turned to face them.

"Aren't you the pretty one, cheeks all rosy like a flower. Perhaps you had a caller, huh?...maybe a gentleman," he taunted her as the men roared with laughter.

"Oh, it is a pity, it is too bad about your friend," he sighed.

"Yes, we came upon him on the road above...but, it is so sad...Hank mistook him for a deer."

"You, you didn't," cried Jenny in distress. "Please tell me you didn't shoot him," she pleaded in terror, putting her hands to her flushed cheeks.

Jacque just stood there, enjoying her moment of terror with a sly smirk on his face.

"No, sadly he missed," laughed Jacque as he threw himself down at the table with a heavy thud. His friends laughing loudly joined him at the table whole heartedly approving his sarcastic wit.

"Bring us something to eat," roared Jacque still laughing. It was apparent they had all been drinking.

"And make it quick, you ugly prune," he added slamming his fist on the table.

"She don't look like no prune to me," retorted one of Jacque's cronies all the while leering at Jenny with a lustful drunken smile on his iniquitous face.

"Shut up!" yelled Jacque, "You stupid swine...you know nothing."

"You are the stupid one," declared the man, "Maybe you cannot see so well, hey?"

"I see that you are aching for a belt in the face," yelled Jacque as he bounded over the table and grabbed the unsuspecting agitator by the throat and shoved him against the rough floor.

"Get out! Get out! All of you!" he ranted waving his arms frantically. "Get out of my house you fools, idiots...that's what you all are...idiots."

They feared Jacque when he was drunk and angry and stumbling over each other they all made a hasty and unceremonious departure. They knew Jacque was capable of brute violence or even murder if necessary.

"Where's my supper?" He snarled at Jenny as he sat back down on the bench.

Jenny placed a bowl of rabbit stew before him on the table and left returning with biscuits and a glass of milk.

"Milk," he growled, "what do I want with sissy food. Bring me some of that whiskey I brought home last week," he commanded, "unless you've taken to drinking it yourself, but no, you are not woman enough," he jeered.

"By the way," he continued, "when we stopped old man Schultz on the road to see what he was up to, he told me he had come here to see about buying the calf...is that true?" questioned Jacque while looking at Jenny out of his blood–shot eyes.

Mr. Schultz had said nothing to her about the calf. What could she say in response to his question?

"No matter," smirked Jacque, "I told him he could take both the cow and the calf. I even threw in the chickens. He'll pick them up tomorrow morning."

Jenny felt cold fingers of fear go up her spine. Jacque was up to something and it sent great fear into her heart, especially for her young children. The cow and the calf along with a few chickens had been on the farm when they arrived from St. Louis.

Thankfully, they had been a source of food as Jacque provided little in that respect.

Won't we be needing the cow and chickens?" asked Jenny in a soft almost inaudible voice.

"Speak up so I can hear you, you...frump," shouted Jacque, "and how do you expect me to eat this swill? It's not fit for pigs," and with one sweep of his arm he pushed the food across the table and onto the floor.

"Clean it up, you...you trash," he yelled, "you crazy daughter of a bar maid."

As Jenny bent over quickly to pick up the mess, Jacque suddenly kicked her from behind and sent her smashing into the wall. Before she could move, he grabbed her by the hair,

which had fallen down around her shoulders and threw her
hard against the kitchen cabinet. Most of its contents went
crashing onto the hard dirt floor. His rage wasn't consumed,
but at that moment, Robbie came flying from behind the
curtain, which separated the children's bed from the living
area. He pounded Jacque with his little fists, and kicked him
with all the force his seven year old body could muster. Jenny
felt sure Jacque would finish them both off right then and there.
Instead, he grabbed the kicking and flailing child and held him
up in the air for a moment. He then dropped him with a thud on
the floor and turned to stagger across the room where he fell on
top of the other bed.

Jenny could see that Elizabeth, her six year old, had
pulled aside the curtain and was staring out in fear. She
motioned for her to go back.

Jacque soon begin to snore.

"Are you alright, Ma, Ma?" questioned Robbie, his lips
trembling, but his jaw held tight and firm.

"Yes, I think so," whispered Jenny, although she wasn't
sure. Every bone in her body hurt, but her concern was for
Robbie.

Finally, after some moments, Jenny moved to shut and
bolt the door. She feared Jacque's friends more than the heat
and was afraid they might stray back inside. She was sure they
had gone only as far as the barn.

Robbie tip–toed over and got the broom and together
they worked in silence cleaning up the broken glass.

Elizabeth had slipped out of bed and was now attempting
to help but Jenny waved her back so she wouldn't cut her feet
on the glass. She looked so much like Jenny with her long
copper colored curls and soft white complexion.

They finished with hardly a sound and slipped into bed
with sleeping baby Jacqueline, who was still fast asleep.

Sometime in the night sleep finally overcame Jenny and
she was not aware that Jacque and his men rose early and rode
off. When she awoke, they were gone.

Early that morning, in the dark stillness of the room, as
the rain fell softly outside, Jenny called out to her God. For a

long time now, she had not been able to do so, but now she needed to so desperately.

"Oh, God," she sobbed, "I need your help. Oh, please forgive me. Help my children. What can I do... where can I go that Jacque will not find us? I know I have let the grief in my heart, because of David's death and this tragic marriage to Jacque, drive me away from you...but, Lord God, I desperately need you...Oh, I need you. Please help me," she cried.

"David and I were so happy together and it was he who lead me to you, Jesus, O Sweet Jesus. I have no understanding of why David was taken from us but I must not question anymore. Instead, I vow to trust you. I pray you will forgive me and somehow, in some way lead us safely away from this place."

As Jenny paced back and forth across the dirt floor still praying, she watched as a small bit of morning light tried to slip between the rain clouds and push through the small yellowed window. Looking down through her tears her teary eyes focused on something.

"What?" Jenny whispered picking it up and carrying the shiny heart shaped locket toward the dim light of the window. She was amazed at its presence for she had never seen it before. She held it up and opened it. Inside was a picture of a beautiful young woman and a little girl. Forgetting her prayers, she pulled the small picture from the locket. On the back it read, "To Jenna with love, mother," and underneath the inscription, "Boston, Massachusetts, 18..." the year was smudged. Across the back of the locket was engraved the name, "Gordon."

She turned and looked, searching the floor where the chaos had taken place the night before. She thought she had cleaned everything up, but there under the cabinet still laid her most precious possession, her mothers box. In it was all she knew of the past existence of her mother. But Jenny had never seen this locket. Picking up the plain wooden box she saw how it had broken in the calamity revealing a compartment where the locket had been hidden. Still inside she found some letters and a picture of two young women, one of whom might have been her mother, Paulette.

"Why?" What was so important about this locket that her mother had to hide it?" whispered Jenny to herself.

"What does it mean, Lord?" Jenny questioned thoughtfully.

She felt a new surge of joy and she didn't understand why. Suddenly, she felt that all of her answers lay somewhere in Boston...it cut deep into her heart.

"Boston, Massachusetts," Jenny let the words roll off her bruised lips.

She held the picture up to the light again. Who were these mysterious people...perhaps her mother as a child? Undoubtedly, this was the child's mother, whoever they might be. There was something about them that made her feel that they were devoted to one another, and Jenny felt drawn to them.

It was something Jenny and Paulette, her mother, had never experienced. Could it be that Paulette had regarded someone with that kind of tender affection long ago. If so what had happened to change her so much and had caused her to become the cold and unfeeling person Jenny had known her to be.

Carefully she pulled open the letters, but their contents remained a mystery as they were written in French, Paulettes' native language.

A tear rolled down Jenny's cheek as she gently placed the locket back into the secret folds of the box along with the other articles and closed the lid. She briefly held the box tenderly to her breast.

The chaos of another fearful night with Jacque melted away for a few glorious seconds as Jenny stood in the fading light of the overcast sky.

Somehow, the locket gave her the first feelings of identity of belonging...something she had never felt before.

David had always said, "All things in His time," and Jenny knew this was God's way of saying it is time.

"Almost, well yes," laughed Jenny joyfully, proclaiming out loud, "It's time! Yes it's time to leave this place."

Chapter Two

Robbie, please look down the road again and see if Mr. Schultz is coming," said Jenny.

She doubted that Jacque's story of selling the cow and calf this morning were true. He would do or say anything to unsettle her nerves. Even if it was so, Mr. Schultz may not have taken him seriously. Hopefully, Jenny had sent Robbie up the road twice now, just in case he might come by.

Robbie ran out the door, around the house and up the hill to the road again. The water from the river was unmistakably rising closer to the house now, but the road had been established away from the river on higher ground beyond the house.

"Elizabeth," called Jenny, "come and help mama. Here put these folded clothes into this satchel and then please help Jacqueline get dressed."

She noticed Jacqueline wasn't doing too well on her own.

"Time, time," stammered Jenny as she hastened to slice a loaf of bread. Hurriedly she smoothed soft golden butter across each crusty slice. She filled a bottle with cool spring water from the bucket on the stand and wrapped it in Jacqueline's small quilt to keep it cool.

"Matches," she mumbled, "and candles," she was trying so hard not to forget essentials.

"Elizabeth, I asked you to put these clothes in the satchel," admonished Jenny, realizing the folded pile still remained on the chair where she had placed them. "Why didn't you do it?" she questioned annoyingly.

"I'm sorry mama," answered the child, "but I dressed Jacqueline first," she looked at her mother for approval.

Jenny could see that Elizabeth had three year old Jacqueline nearly dressed, except for her shoes. She was in the process of pulling them on now. "You did good," smiled Jenny. She knew there were times when she expected too much from the children in spite of their young age. Reaching with one hand, she rubbed the back of her neck. She tried to calm herself. She had made such a drastic decision. A decision to leave and it was of the utmost importance that they go now before Jacque and his men returned. It was a desperate thought but how she hoped Mr. Schultz would come. She had no money but if he would pay them for the stock before Jacque returned, it might be enough to take them to St. Louis. It was her money too, although Jacque wouldn't see it that way. Well, no matter, they were leaving and that was final.

"She's dressed, Mama. I'll fill the satchel now," declared Elizabeth.

"Never mind, Honey," said Jenny, "I've got it. Just watch Jacqueline for me and find her rag doll, please."

Jenny packed anxiously but with great vigilance, being aware that what she took may have to last them for an unknown length of time.

I guess that will be it, she said to herself as she realized that the bulging satchel was crammed to the full.

"Oh, my—my mother's box, " she cried, "I almost forgot it."

Carefully she picked up the precious box and making room for it placed it within he satchel. Earlier she had retrieved the letter from its' secret place behind the cabinet.

"Where is that boy?" Jenny mumbled to herself as she took one last look about the place to make sure she hadn't forgotten anything. A clash of thunder sent her hurrying to the door.

"Robbie," she called loudly. "Robbie, where are you?"

The boy suddenly appeared from around the side of the house leading the cow and calf. He had brought them down the slope from the barn.

"I thought I might as well bring them from the stable while I was up there," he stated, hoping he had made the right decision

"But why Robbie?" asked Jenny with some annoyance, feeling sure by now that Mr. Schultz was not coming.

"He's almost here, Mama. I can tell it's him. I can see him coming from the top of the hill," assured the boy.

"Are you positive it's him?" questioned Jenny, fearful of Jacque's soon unexpected return

"Yes, Mama, I can tell it's him," asserted the boy. "Are...are we going someplace, Mama?" questioned Robbie staring at the satchel in the doorway where Jenny had placed it.

"Come here, children," said Jenny sternly, yet kindly.

"I need to tell you something very important, and you must listen to me carefully. It is because I love you all so much, that we must leave the farm today.

"Is Jacque coming too?" questioned Elizabeth with a fearful look on her pretty face.

"Shhh," admonished Robbie, "don't interrupt Mama. Is that what the suitcase is for?" he asked.

"No, Jacque is not coming with us, Elizabeth," answered Jenny. Then turning to Robbie she continued, "As soon as Mr. Schultz comes for the cow we will leave," she informed him.

"He's here, Mama. He's here," pointed the boy with excitement as the bulky figured man swung the big team of horses in from the road.

"Hello, Mrs. Boshart, I wanted to talk with you about the cow and calf," he said as he jumped down from the wagon and drew closer.

"Is the mister at home?" he questioned while cautiously looking around.

"No, he left early this morning," explained Jenny.

"Well your husband put some real pressure on me to tell him why I had been to your house last night. We met on the road just shortly after I left here. Maybe I did the wrong thing but I had a funny feelin' I shouldn't tell him about that letter," he said while dropping his eyes toward the ground and spitting sideways toward some bushes. "I don't like liars Mrs. Boshart, but I reckon I told one to your husband. Yep, I told him I came here to see about buying that calf. It was something I was wantin' to do, but I never figured he'd sell it to me." He spit again and then looked sheepishly at Jenny.

"I am sorry if its gonna cause you any hardship. The mister told me to take the both of them, plus the chickens," he explained looking toward the cow and calf, "but I won't take any of them if you don't have a mind for me to."

"That will be fine," insisted Jenny trying not to belay her nervousness. "They are ready to go. You can take them now and I understand what you are saying and appreciate what you did," she smiled a faint smile.

"Well, that's another thing," he replied, "I've been waitin' for this weather to clear so's I could make a trip to town. We're gettin' mighty low on supplies. It don't seem like it's gettin' much better, so's I thought I'd take a chance and make a try at it today. If all goes well, I should be back before dark. I could just stop and get them on my way back through here tonight.

"You're going into town?" interrupted Jenny.

"Yes, " he continued, "but I'll pay you now the amount your husband and I agreed on. I'll just tie them to the back of the wagon on my way through here later. I brought a crate for the chickens."

"That would be fine. That would be just wonderful, but Mr. Schultz, would it be alright for me and the children to ride into town with you?" asked Jenny. "My husband has gone away for a few days. I think we are in real danger of flooding if we stay here," she said gesturing toward the river. "I'm really worried about the water rising and I think we should feel safer in town," she explained. What she was saying she felt was true, there was no need to explain further to Mr. Schultz.

I sure can't disagree with you there," he said, shaking his head in disbelief. "I ain't never seen that river rise like that. If only this rain would let up." Then feeling into his pocket he pulled out the agreed upon purchase money for the animals and giving it to Jenny said, "It will be just fine for you to ride with me into town."

"I would like to leave as soon as possible though," he added. "Will you be ready to go soon?"

Another clap of thunder sounded overhead. The air was heavy, but for the first time in days, it had actually stopped raining, at least for the moment. "I'm afraid we are in for more bad weather," he said scowling up at the clouds. "Just wish it would hold off for a few more hours. Wife wouldn't come with me. Said she wouldn't come out in this heat. Don't blame her, although she hates to miss a trip to town. Don't blame you either for wantin' to get yourself and the little ones away from this river bottom. Better hurry now," he suggested.

"We're just about ready," said Jenny, elated that they had a ride into town.

"I'll just take the cow and calf back up to the stable for you so's we can get on our way. Boy, you help you mother get ready," said the man

Mr. Schultz had no more than gone around the side of the house when Jenny shooed the children toward the wagon. The big horses were stomping their feet and pawing at the soggy ground. The heat and flies were making them behave wildly. Elizabeth jumped back as a tail came switching over her head.

"It's all right, Elizabeth," said Jenny assuredly.

She tried to help the children into the wagon but winced with pain from the bruised shoulder. Robbie gave Elizabeth a boost and then with a little effort lifted Jacqueline over the side into the wagon bottom. Jenny carefully lifted the satchel and dropped it into the wagon. By the time Jenny had seated herself on one of the crates in the back, Mr. Schultz had returned and climbed upon the seat behind the horses.

"Ready to go?" he shouted back over his shoulder. "All aboard then," and he gave a starting jerk to the reins. The horses bolted upright throwing the wagon about wildly. The children screamed and clung to Jenny.

"It's okay," yelled Mr. Schultz over the noise of the horses and wagon. "Quite down, Babe, whoa girl," he yelled as he tried to calm the troubled team. "I sure am sorry," he shouted back as he got the horses under control. "They're acting daft. Animals just go crazy in this heat. Everyone all right back there?" he wanted to know.

"We're just fine," Jenny yelled back as she settled the children. "I know you have a bump Elizabeth, but it will be okay in a minute. Just sit down in the wagon and when we get into town, Mama will buy you all a peppermint stick." The children quietly obeyed, the promise of a peppermint stick was like Christmas and birthdays all thrown together.

"How far is it to town?" shouted Jenny to Mr. Schultz over the noise of the wagon. In the year they had lived on the farm Jacque had not allowed them to go anywhere. He would not permit the children to even go to school. Visitors for Jenny were out of the question although the Schultz's had come a few times without his knowledge. Jacque brought in what supplies he thought they needed. She and the children had lived as though they were prisoners.

"Well, if we don't run into any trouble," yelled Mr. Schultz, "we should be there before noon."

How wonderful, thought Jenny to herself to actually be in town with people by noon. Away from the farm, away from the water and the loneliness...but most of all away from Jacque and his awful beatings. She smiled a little smile and slid herself down off the crate onto the bottom of the wagon using the crate to brace her back some. Her shoulder throbbed and she was sure Mr. Schultz could not have helped to see her discolored face. Her lip was cut and somewhat swollen, but he was either too much of a gentleman to ask her about it or else the weather had completely distracted him. She knew he had seen her that way a couple of times before, but had never let on. Robbie seemed fine in spite of the fearful situation he had endured last night. Jenny determined in her mind to never let anything like that happen to him again

"Dear Lord," she prayed silently, "please get us safely away from this place."

As the wagon jostled along the rough road and the children played in the wagon bottom, Jenny's mind wandered back to her childhood. Its dark and mysterious corridors troubled her. She and her mother had not been close, far from it. Jenny never called her mother, she only knew her as Paulette. She supplied Jenny's basic needs; clothing, ample food and schooling. Jenny had considered her mother to be attractive, but always distant, showing no affection toward her. At times

Jenny felt that Paulette hated her. She tried to please Paulette, but to no avail. Paulette was churlish and sharp tongued with Jenny, but a more genial self toward the patrons of the bar. They had lived over a tavern and Jenny suspected that selling drinks wasn't her only occupation. She also had a problem with alcohol, which grew worse as time went by. They lived together with a couple of other ladies of like occupation to whom Jenny felt closer at times than she did to her own mother.

Paulette became upset easily and would rant and rave in French as she threw things about. She died when Jenny was about twelve. Jenny's definite age and who her father had been were questions she feared to ask. She never celebrated a birthday and Paulette furnished no information as to her father's identity. When Paulette became ill, Jenny cared for her as best she could. They were allowed to stay in the space above the tavern if Jenny worked in the kitchen. Because the tavern was on the main thoroughfare, it also served good hearty food. Jenny had found the kitchen to be a warm friendly haven. Pierre, the cook, had long ago became a friend to the sad little girl with the red–brown hair. She had been so shy and afraid when she first begin to stop by the kitchen on her way home from school. But Pierre was so kind to her that before long, not only was she watching the preparation of food as Pierre introduced here to the fine culinary art of cooking, but she found a place of comfort in that kitchen and after some time, became an excellent cook herself.

As Paulette's condition grew worse and she was confined to bed, Jenny would sit for long evenings silently by her bedside. Sometimes if Paulette felt strong enough, Jenny would brush her long dark hair. Toward the end, she seemed to soften some toward Jenny and even to appreciate the attention that was so lovingly given. Paulette lapsed in and out of consciousness as her days drew to an end. The last day of her life as Jenny set beside her, Paulette raised herself and pointed to the dresser.

"In my drawer," she gasped for breath, "in my drawer is a box…get it for me."

Jenny went to the dresser, opened the drawer, and rummaged through its contents until she found a small wooden box.

"Is this what you want?" she asked as she brought it back to the bed obediently.

"Yes, it is yours. Take it," she said as she pushed it weakly away...she closed her eyes and dropped back on the pillow. She never spoke again. She was gone in a matter of hours.

If it had not been for Pierre, the cook, Jenny's dear friend, she was sure her own life might have ended then also. With the death of her mother, she had no place to go.

Pierre, the two ladies, and Pete, the owner of the tavern, had passed a hat around the bar and taken up enough money for a funeral. It was Pierre who talked Pete into letting Jenny stay on and work in the kitchen with him. This gave her a place to live and something to eat and that was about it. School was over for Jenny, she never returned.

Large rain drops falling on her face suddenly awoke Jenny from her memories.

"Mama, it's raining hard," said Robbie shaking Jenny's arm to get her attention.

"Me all wet, Mama, " chortled Jacqueline as little rivulets of water ran down her chubby cheeks, her blonde hair all curly and tumbled. Even baby Jacqueline seemed happy to get away from the farm as she paddy–caked her hands together delighted with the rain.

Chapter Three

Jenny realized the horses had come to a stop.

"Mrs. Boshart, it's getting real bad. The team is getting bogged down in the mud and it looks worse ahead," explained Mr. Schultz as he jumped down from the wagon.

Jenny could see nothing but water running across the road about thirty feet ahead. It looked like quite a stretch of it was covered and hard to tell how deep it was.

"It looks like I got to turn back. I haven't got any other choice," he said as he looked in dismay at the rising water. I guess I should have tried to make it through yesterday."

"Mama, are we going back?" asked Robbie. "I don't want to go back," he said trying to hold back the tears.

Elizabeth realizing they may be returning home began to fuss about not getting her peppermint stick in town.

"Elizabeth, stop that!" said Jenny, "We will get your candy. Just be good children so we can decide what to do."

What to do...what to do, she thought to herself. Lord can you hear me...we can't go back. Her mind was racing to find a solution.

"I think I can make it back as far as your place," Mr. Schultz tried to explain as he mopped his face with his big red handkerchief. "I'll go back and get the cow and take the road that swings to higher ground from there. It wouldn't be right for me to leave you and the little one's with the river rising. My wife would never forgive me. So's you all just better come home with me until we see what this weather is going to do."

"That's really kind of you," said Jenny, but she knew that wasn't far enough away from Jacque.

"Is there any other way to get to town?" questioned Jenny while pushing a strand of wet hair back from her face. She had fastened it in a bun that morning, but the rain and humidity had partially pulled it down. She tried to re–pin it as Mr. Schultz stood there thinking.

"Well," he answered with skepticism, "Yes, there is an old trail that juts off from this road. It cuts off up through the woods and hills. Since this good road has been in along the flat land, no one ever much uses it. As far as I know, it still goes all the way into town. Old Barney Howes still does a lot of trappin' and I remember a few months back him saying the trail was still usable. I think he had him a cabin up there somewhere. But Mrs. Bochart, you wouldn't be thinkin' about tryin' to take those children up through that rough country, would you?" he questioned, shaking his head in disbelief. "There's wolves up in those hills. My gracious you're not big enough yourself to hike off into them wilds alone."

"Mr. Schultz," Jenny interrupted, throwing up her hands as if to stop him, "We are not going back! If there is any way at all we can get through, we must try. Now, please," she said, "say no more. You will frighten the children. We can make it. We will just stay on the trail and keep going until we get to town. Now," she questioned, "where does this trail begin?"

There wasn't anything Mr. Schultz could do to change Jenny's mind. It was made up for certain, and in a way, he understood. Too many times, he had witnessed how Jacque had mistreated his family. Still he felt responsible for Jenny and the children's safety, but if they did not move quickly the wagon would be mired in mud.

"The trail is back about a half mile or so, if I can find it in this rain," he said, resigning himself to the idea he had done all he could do. He jumped back up on the wagon seat and turned the big team successfully around. They sloshed off in the direction of the farm. It wasn't long before he brought the team to a halt again.

"This is it Mrs. Boshart, Believe me," he said, "I'd take you through with the horses but as you can see it's too overgrown and narrow. Sure you won't change your mind and come home with me?" he almost pleaded.

"I really appreciate your thoughtfulness," she said, but Jenny was determined and she slid herself down from the safety of the wagon and reached for the satchel. Mr. Schultz came back and helped the children down.

"Anything else I can do for you ma'am?" he asked sadly as Jenny reached out her small hand to thank him.

"No, you have been most kind," she answered. "I pray you can get the cow and make it home safely yourself."

"God bless you," he said.

Jenny wanted to tell Mr. Schultz that if he saw Jacque anywhere soon, please do not to tell him where they had gone. But somehow, she just couldn't put that burden on the kindly old man or embarrass herself by asking him to do that.

They waved goodbye as they started through the woods. The trail was surrounded by thick foliage and woods on both sides. The rain had let up some again; it had been like that, it seemed, for days. Never–ending, intermittent showers, sometimes heavier than others.

"Me can't see," fretted Jacqueline.

Jenny had taken the satchel by one hand and the baby's hand in the other letting the little girl walk at her own pace. Robbie and Elizabeth held hands tightly as they followed a few steps behind their mother.

"Alright," laughed Jenny, trying to relieve any fear the children might have about the trip through the wet woods.

"I'm going to get down and let you on my back. I will be your horse. But you must be very careful as your horse has a very bad shoulder," Jenny cautioned Jacqueline.

"Oh," squealed the little girl in delight, "a horsey ride...a horsey ride," as she climbed as gently as she could on Jenny's back.

"Hold on tight now, as I have to carry the satchel," explained Jenny.

"I will. Get up horsey," she giggled as she wrapped her little legs around Jenny's midriff and her arms about her neck.

It wasn't too bad thought Jenny. They just kept walking in the direction the trail took them. Robbie and Elizabeth seemed almost to be enjoying themselves. They had not been away from the farm in all the time they had lived there, so it was rather fun for the two. They talked away to each other stopping now and then to pick up a stone or a pretty leaf. The drizzle of rain began again.

The trail had widened out to about three or four feet now with mostly bushes and trees along the way, but sometimes they would come into a clearing and the trail would take them to a sort of a meadow. Jenny liked it when the trees would clear and she could see her surroundings better. Mostly, it seemed they wound their way slowly up hill away from the flooding river bottom. After sometime Robbie and Elizabeth's pace grew slower and slower, especially the little girl.

"Mama, Elizabeth keeps stopping," lamented Robbie as they turned a curve and came into a little clearing.

"I'm thirsty," said Elizabeth, "can we have a drink?"

"How about lunch?" answered Jenny. Her shoulder was tired and Jacqueline was growing heavy.

They found a place somewhat dry under a big tree just off the trail in a little clearing. They sat down on the heaved up roots of the tree as Jenny gave them all a drink of water and large slices of bread and butter. They tried to rest, Jenny with her back against the tree, but the heat was relentless and the bugs were worse. Not wanting to spend the night on the trail, they started off again.

Robbie decided that he would carry the satchel for awhile giving Jenny some much needed relief. Jacqueline wanted to walk but she was too slow so in order to make any time, Jenny became her horse again. Every time they rounded a curve and came over the crest of a knoll, Jenny hoped to see town. She had no timepiece and the sky was so overcast and dreary it was difficult to tell what time it was. It seemed that they had been on the trail forever. It must be late afternoon, she thought. The children were exhausted and so was she. Perhaps they had taken a wrong turn. Jenny had tried to stay on the main trail, but a couple of times they had been uncertain which way to go when side paths would veer off from the main trail. The path had become rocky and steep on the downside now with hilly woods rising high on the other.

Jenny didn't like the looks of the sky at all as the little group rounded yet another curve and they were met with a sharp streak of lightning. Jenny never liked lightning—she never liked storms.

"Oh, I can't believe this!" she cried out in tired desperation. "Lord, where are you? Oh, give me strength," she prayed. "I don't think I can endure much more," she wept.

She stopped and wiped her tears with one hand. She could not show fear for the sake of the children. Thunder crashed and rumbled through the atmosphere. The wind now picked up with a fierceness and the sky was no longer dreary gray, but black.

All that Jenny could think was that if they had not strayed off the trail, and then town must not be too far away. It seemed they had walked all day but they must keep going. True, they hadn't been able to walk very fast and they had stopped to eat, but Mr. Schultz had thought they should make it by late afternoon.

The only thing that Jenny could see ahead now though were trees and a sheet of rain heading straight for them. It had turned so dark, that except for the jagged flashes of lightning they could hardly make their way along the path. The force of the wind now made it impossible to make any headway.

Jenny put Jacqueline down on the wet ground, where she clung to her mother in fear and raised her arms high in the air, her shoulder hurting mercilessly.

"Oh, God!" she screamed as loud as she could above the storm. "Can you hear me? Can you see Robbie and Elizabeth and the baby? They have done nothing wrong. I beg you, forgive me Lord for my mistakes…" weeping she went on, "please, please! Help us now! Deliver us from this storm and from, Jacque." That was all she had strength left to do.

Jenny reached down and picked up Jacqueline in her arms. She felt a little better. The storm was just as violent, maybe even worse, but the terrible fear had subsided within her. Even the pain in her shoulder seemed quieted. Elizabeth and Robbie were clinging to her drenched skirt.

"What's that, Mama?" yelled Robbie pointing toward the woods off the side of the trail just ahead.

"What, Robbie? What did you see?" shouted Jenny with her heart pounding wildly again.

"It looked like a little house," said Robbie straining his eyes to see through the rain. "Look, there it is! Did you see it in that flash of lightning?"

"Yes, yes, I did," Jenny cried excitedly with much relief. "Oh, maybe we have made it to town. Come on children."

They tried to run against the wind and the rain as it lashed and buffeted them about. Elizabeth fell twice, but Robbie with a firm grip managed to pull her along with him.

It was a little house, a log cabin of some sort. No matter of pounding on the door brought any results. The solid wooden door was padlocked from the outside. Jenny tried to push open one of the glass windows on either side of the door, but they were locked also. Certain she had no choice if she was to get them out of the elements, in the next flash of light she grabbed a large tree limb and broke the glass of a window pain. Clearing away the glass from the window ledge, she squeezed herself into the cabin.

"Robbie, hand me the satchel," she commanded.

Quickly she found matches and a candle. Lighting the candle she could see the cabin consisted of a single large room and there was no one there.

"Here, Robbie, hand Jacqueline in to me," she directed. With Jacqueline inside, Elizabeth and then Robbie were quickly drawn into the dry room out of the storm.

It was a well–built cabin with a solid roof and floor. Jenny would be happy to exchange it for the house on the farm any day. The only windows and door were in the wall they had just entered. There were two bunk beds built against the rough–hewn log wall. Some cupboards lined the back of the room. There was a table with two chairs. Jenny had noticed a kerosene lamp on the table. It looked like it was in working condition, so lighting the wick and adjusting the flame, she made a soft glow throughout the room.

"I think God just answered our prayers," said Jenny as she smiled happily at the children.

They looked so tired, so weary, and wet. But, thank God, they were out of the storm and away from the terror of Jacque for the night. If the owner returned before morning, she would just explain some of what happened and pay him for the window. She would certainly leave money behind to pay for the broken window before they left in the morning.

They exchanged their wet things for dry clothes from the satchel. Jenny wiped the dust as best she could from the table and set out what food they had. She even found a can of beans in the cupboard and with a little searching, a can opener, some tin plates, and cups. They were hungry and it looked like a feast set before them.

Jacqueline was soon fast asleep on her mother's lap. Jenny spread the quilt on the floor, as the beds had nothing in them but hard boards. Elizabeth and Robbie didn't need any coaxing to join their sister in much needed rest.

Jenny was somewhat concerned about the open window. They had often left their windows open in the heat of a summer's night, but it was just they had no idea where they were and what dangers lurked outside the cabin. She found a piece of torn cloth in the bottom of the cupboard; however, she couldn't secure it over the opening, as the wind and rain were too strong. It was hot anyway, and even if a little rain came in, it was a small window and the air felt good.

The light from the lamp seemed to give her comfort from her fear of the storm and darkness. Still, she felt it was best to turn it out. She wanted to stay awake but her body was just too physically exhausted. She took the candle and matches and lay close beside the sleeping children.

"Thank you, Lord," she breathed softly as she drifted off to sleep.

Chapter Four

Jenny woke with a start! It was very dark. The rain seemed to have stopped and the wind to have stilled. She felt she was half in a dream world of unreality, trying to focus her mind on something that had jolted her awake. Perhaps she had only been dreaming. Oh, it's hot thought Jenny trying to clear her mind. The air hung heavy and humid. Still that wasn't what had disturbed her sleep and caused her sudden awareness of something, but what?

No, it was a sound. What was it? Then she heard it again. She wasn't dreaming. With her heart pounding, she listened—something closer now—outside the wall of the cabin.

Slowly and with tenderness, in spite of her fear, Jenny moved the sleeping Jacqueline from beside her. The baby stirred and whimpered as she moved her.

"Shh," comforted Jenny, patting the sleeping child gently.

"What's wrong Mama?" asked Robbie sleepily. "Are you alright? I thought I heard a funny noise."

"I did too," whispered Jenny, "shh, just listen."

"Mama, where are you?" whimpered Elizabeth. "I can't see it's so dark. I think I'm melting. It's so hot I can't breave."

"Hush, Elizabeth, I think there is someone outside of the cabin," said Jenny with as much calmness as she could pretend.

She picked up the candles and matches and made her way toward the broken window. As she neared the open space, she heard something brush roughly against the outside of the wall. Oh, let it be a raccoon or even a skunk, she thought to herself. Please don't let it be Jacque. Every nerve of her body vibrated with terror as a long guttural sound arose from the throat of whatever was on the other side of the wall. Panic raced through her mind, she could only hope whatever it was would not try or be able to enter through the open window.

She waited—if only her heart would stop pounding so hard. From somewhere out along the ridge of the trail came a long shrill howl. Jenny had heard that sound many times before, but it never ceased to send cold chills up and down her spine. She had never heard them this close. Usually, they stayed far away from the clearings and inhabited areas, but it was so hot that as Mr. Schultz had said, "The animals were crazy with the heat." Jacque had told her they were coyotes, but they sounded like wolves to Jenny.

Another howl came from further away as if in answer to the first. She waited—holding her breath—then one came so close that for a moment Jenny thought the inside of the cabin had already been invaded. She had to get herself under control. Stop shaking! She told herself. Fear go away! Think rationally. Pray. What was that scripture she had learned when she first met David?... "For God hath not given us the Spirit of fear, but of power and love, and of a sound mind."

Again, something suddenly caught her attention. It was the sound of brushing and scraping against the side of the cabin directly in front of the absent windowpane. Quickly, she lit a match, but as she tried to catch the wick of the candle with the flame, the flickering match lighted the window area just enough to let Jenny look full into the gleaming, yellow eyes of a large wolf–like animal. Its' teeth were bared as it pulled its' mouth back in a savage snarl and let out a ghastly growl. Its' front paws were braced on the windowsill as if to propel itself into the room.

Jenny could not stifle the scream that arose from her throat as the flame from the match faded away. Hurriedly, she tried with shaking hands to light another match. They were damp, but this time somehow she was successful in lighting the candle and then gingerly she held it up to the open space of the window. The animal was gone. She took a quick glance about the cabin to be sure it hadn't slipped through the opening when the match went out. It looked all right. The children were much awake, badly frightened, but trying to be still, or perhaps too afraid to move. Robbie had drawn them to the back wall as far away from the window as he could.

"Robbie," spoke Jenny with a quavering voice, "quickly bring me the lamp from the table.

He ran and quickly brought the lamp to her while inquiring, "Did it go away, Mama?"

"I don't know," she answered, "bring me a chair."

Suddenly it was back panting and jumping, trying to get a foothold from which to push its self into the cabin. Jenny lighted the kerosene lamp and raised the wick as high as it would go, then she jerked off the lantern top and pushed the flaming lamp into the window just as the huge animal thrust its head into the opening. It retreated as if someone had struck it with a whip. She could hear it yelping off into the woods behind the cabin.

"Get away! Get away! Get out of here!" Jenny screamed after it. Replacing the lantern top, she steadied the lamp in the window. She feared the animal might be rabid. She waited thinking to use the chair as a weapon if it returned. After some time she looked to see the children huddled together, silently waiting.

"I think it must be close to daybreak," Jenny told them, "and I believe when light comes they will go away," she explained, wondering if what she was saying had any truth in it.

Very soon, she could see color starting to show in the sky—night begin to slowly slide away as the morning rays of light overpowered the darkness. O, beautiful, glorious sunlight—the first she had seen in days. The lamp still glowed in her hand. She lowered it and took a quick look of surveillance from the window.

"I think they are gone," she said aloud, "and it has stopped raining. The sun is out."

Jenny wondered what time the sun came up—maybe five-o-clock or so. She wasn't sure, but how she would like to free herself and the children from this place—away where there were other people. Early last night the cabin seemed like a haven but now it felt as if they were trapped. She couldn't even open the door from the inside. Their only way of escape was through the window and what was on the other side she wondered. If they left the safety of the cabin, they might be torn apart by the wolves. They could not stay there and wait for help, perhaps to be found by Jacque.

"I think," said Jenny, "that it is a sunny day and we will get an early start. So let's pack up and have breakfast in town."

The children were ready to go. They didn't mind leaving at all. Jenny left what she thought would pay for the broken window and the few things they had used. She left no note of explanation.

Jenny feared what might be waiting for her as she lowered herself from the window, but her greater fear was that Jacque may have returned and found them gone. Perhaps he would persuade Mr. Schultz to tell him about the trail they had taken and by now, he could be in hot pursuit. It wasn't that they mattered in any way to him it was just that he was so devilish that he would make them suffer for leaving without his permission. He had told Jenny that if she ever left him he would find her and the children. Then they would sorely and permanently regret that decision.

The wolves terrified Jenny, but her fear of Jacque was much greater.

As she stepped foot on the wet ground, she could see the muddy marks of large paw prints all around the front of the cabin. She shivered even though it was warm and looked around her wondering if they were lying in the brush somewhere or crouching low ready to attack. She saw nothing. Everything seemed still. Even the wind was quiet.

She left the children in the safety of the cabin.

"I'll be right back," she assured them as she walked over the trail.

"Well, what do you know," she exclaimed to herself in surprise, for just below the rocky ridge of the trail, spread out in full view, was Kansas City. They had made it after all. Now, if they could just go safely down the trail without encountering any of last nights' unfriendly beasts.

In a frenzy of joy she rushed back to the cabin, shouting, "Children, it looks safe, now. Town is just below us. It's probably not more than a mile away."

With as much haste as they could muster, Jenny helped them climb from the cabin and they hurried off down the path. After a short time, they left the ridge as the trail met up with the highway. Soon there were houses on both sides of the street and as Jenny stopped a minute for breath, she discovered how bad their appearance was. Quickly, she tried to smooth the wrinkles from their clothes and brush down their hair. She wiped a smudge from Jacqueline's cheek and pulled up Elizabeth's socks.

Jenny wasn't aware that high on the bluff above them, two yellow eyes watched their every move. Its' singed hair and fear of fire had sent him into the hills the night before. He was too cowardly to venture into town, but nevertheless he watched them from afar. Too bad he had missed their escape down the trail.

"We're hungry," stated Robbie.

"I know," said Jenny, "but, it's so early, nothing seems to be open."

Just then, a milk wagon came rattling down the street. The old horse automatically stopped in the right places, as the man jumped down and delivered the milk.

"Sir, ah, Mr..." said Jenny shyly as he came back to the street after making a delivery. "Could you direct us to the train station?" she inquired.

The milkman was startled to see the young woman and youngsters out so early in the morning, especially carrying their baggage and looking quite disheveled, even after Jenny's attempt at grooming.

"Well," he said, scratching his head, "the train station you say? It's quite a ways off from here."

Something about the situation, Jenny's bruised face for one thing and the tired look of the children in their rumpled clothes made him aware of their plight. He felt they needed a helping hand.

"Listen, I've got to finish this route, but if you want to climb up into the wagon, well, I go right by the station on my way home and I'll give you all a ride. Easier than trying to tell you how to find it," he assured them.

True to his word, he took them straight to the station. When Jenny tried to pay him, he refused saying that he would hope someone would do as much for his own Mrs. and children, if there was ever a need.

Once inside the station, Jenny went directly to the ticket window.

"Sir, I would like four tickets to St. Louis," she said.

"Sorry" came the reply, "tracks under water—can't help you today."

"What would be the best route to New York City," she asked.

"I don't really have anything going east this morning, Mame, we've got a lot of wash outs. If you want to go west it's not so bad, but east...probably not until late tomorrow or who knows when," he answered, throwing up his hands in disgust at the weather.

"Nothing at all?" sighed Jenny wearily.

"All we've got is a cattle train sitting out there," he explained. "It will be leaving in an hour or so. It's got a caboose, but it's open air."

"Where is it going?" she questioned.

"Well, if it gets there, it's heading for Sedalia," he laughed.

"Is it possible to get a train for St. Louis out of Sedalia?" asked Jenny.

"Maybe, all depends," he responded.

"We'll take four tickets," she said to the ticket agent realizing she had to put as much space between themselves and Jacque as she could.

"Sir, one more thing," she said as he handed her the tickets, "is there a market open close by?"

"Out the door and around the corner," he motioned with his hand.

They were on the caboose of the train long before it pulled out. Jenny had purchased crackers and cheese, fruit, milk and cookies from the market. Actually, the only thing open about the caboose were the windows. True there was no glass, but there were heavy tarps to pull down and fasten like shades. Jenny fastened the back four tarps on either side to keep the wind from blowing so strong once they began to move and pick up speed.

She then spread out the food and they ate breakfast while they waited to leave. It wasn't long before the train started with a couple of jerks and then it began to roll smoothly along the tracks, gradually picking up momentum. Soon the clickity–clack of the wheels and the cool breeze, created by the speed, lulled all three children to sleep.

Jenny laid her head back against the seat and relaxed for the first time in days, maybe even years. She thought of the locket secure in the satchel. In all of the turmoil, she hadn't forgotten.

"I'm going home," she said softly, "I'm going home," as a smile crossed her tired face and she closed her eyes with a sigh.

Chapter Five

Jenny was not aware that she too had drifted off to sleep. Now, as she awoke she had no idea how far they had come. The children were just waking. Jenny breathed a sigh of relief realizing they might have wandered around the railroad card and been hurt while she had slept. Jacqueline was just rousing from Jenny's lap as Robbie and Elizabeth sat up to look around from the seat they shared facing her.

"Where are we?" asked Robbie rubbing his eyes and yawning. As if in answer to the question, the train began to slow its speed.

"I don't know," said Jenny, "but I think we are coming into a town.

"While they had slept it had begun to rain again. The sunshine was gone and it was raining hard. The tarps over the windows seemed to have kept them perfectly dry. Gradually, the train slowed and through the rain, Jenny could see the outline of some buildings. It didn't seem to be a very large town, but it was difficult to tell. She and the children began to gather up their things just as a man in a raincoat and hat came along side the car.

"Sedalia," he shouted, "Everybody off for Sedalia. End of the line…last stop, Sedalia."

Jenny watched him making his way along the row of boxcars checking doors and cars as he went. She could see the station now in the direction he had taken.

"It looks like we'll have to run for it if we don't want to get too wet," she said. "Robbie and Elizabeth, you can carry the satchel." Jenny picked up Jacqueline in her arms and helped the two older children off the train.

As they hurried inside out of the rain, she could see the station was small and deserted except for the ticket agent seated behind his window. She questioned him as to how soon they would be able to get a train for St. Louis or East.

"No train tonight, Mame…some tracks are washed out. A trestle is down and if this rain keeps up, I don't know when a train will be through here," he told her.

"Could you tell me what time it is?" she questioned, having lost all sense of time.

"It's four–thirty in the afternoon," he answered. "Ordinarily, that train would have been here less than half the time. It's a miracle it made it at all. It was getting so late, I figured it was stranded out there someplace. Couldn't believe my ears when I heard it come in. We're closing up for the night as nothing more is coming through now. There's a boarding house across there," he said pointing. "Mostly for cattle and railroad men, but the food's good and it's the only place in town to spend the night."

Jenny had so hoped that they would be able to get through to St. Louis tonight. Having no choice in the matter, they crossed the muddy street and knocked on the door of a large old house. A sign blowing in the wind and rain announced that it was Nellie's Boarding House. It also listed some prices but Jenny couldn't see too well for the rain. She was thankful the porch that stretched across the front of the house had a roof.

She knocked on the door and in a minute a young girl of about sixteen greeted them with, "Hello, what do you want?" while looking rather surprised to see Jenny and the three little ones.

"We would like a room for the night," explained Jenny.

"Ma!" yelled the girl, looking down the hallway, "more boarders. A woman with some little kids. They need a place for the night."

"Well, tell them to come in for goodness sakes," came from a heavy, flushed–faced woman, as she approached them from a nearby room. "Oh, you poor babies!" she exclaimed. "Let me get you some towels. You're dripping wet." She scurried off and soon returned with a couple of large towels. "What are you doing out in the storm with these poor little ones?" she asked while helping Jenny dry them some.

"We're on our way to St. Louis," answered Jenny, "but this is as far as the train could take us tonight—too many tracks washed out I guess."

"That's too bad," lamented the woman, "well, let me show you to your room and you can all change while I finish supper. I hope you've got some dry clothes with you. It don't look like you've got much in that little case. I suppose you got luggage at the station. By the way…" she added as she started up the flight of stairs leading up from the front door in the hallway, "my name is Nellie. I run this place. What's yours?"

"My name is Jenny, came the answer, "and this is my son Robbie and daughters Elizabeth and Jacqueline."

At the top of the stairs, they took a short turn to the right. The room they entered had one large bed. There was a large oval rug on the floor, worn but serviceable. There were two good–sized windows facing the front of the house, which had been left wide open. The curtains were widely blowing about and the rain was soaking the floor.

"Oh, good grief," exclaimed Nellie in distress, "I told Rachel to close all the windows when it first started to rain. What am I ever going to do with that thoughtless girl. Just look at that rug." She slammed the windows down and mopped up the floor with the same towels she had brought to dry the children.

"Rachel is my fifteen–year old daughter," she explained, "you met her at the door. She just never pays any attention to what I tell her any more, all she thinks about is boys. She's probably day dreaming about some boy right now instead of setting the table for supper like she's supposed to, well, enough of my problems. Sure got some cute kids there."

"I'll get a cot in here for the boy soon's supper is over. I'd bring it in now, but I need to get back to the kitchen. You folks do want supper don't you?"

"How much is the room and supper?" questioned Jenny.

Nellie quoted her a price and added "…kids is free as long as they don't waste nothing. I can't abide anybody wasting food."

It seemed agreeable to Jenny, but she hoped the ticket for St. Louis would not be for more than she had left from the money Mr. Schultz had given her.

After combing everyone's hair, changing into what dry clothes they could find and washing hands and faces in the big wash basin on the night–stand, they joined the other boarders in the large old dining room downstairs.

Supper was delicious, fried chicken, creamy mashed potatoes and dumplings and gravy, homemade bread and butter, fresh cooked vegetables, plenty of milk for the children and large glasses of buttermilk for the adults if they cared for it. For dessert, there was homemade apple pie with ample slices of cheese.

Several men were seated at the table. They were dressed in rough work clothes and conversed amongst themselves about cattle and the railroad. There was an elderly lady who was on her way to visit her son somewhere in the west. She talked a little to Jenny, asking the children's names and ages and commented on the weather, but remained silent for most of the meal. There was also a bald–headed little man, dressed in a suit. He said he was a traveling salesman, but he had little else to say. Somehow, every time he looked up it seemed he was staring at her. Jenny felt sorry for him, as he seemed so sad and alone. Rachel and Nellie waited on the table, not sitting down with the guests.

When the meal was finished almost everyone retired to their own rooms, although two or three men wandered into the parlor to relax a while.

It had become apparent even before supper was finished that Nellie and Rachel were arguing about something as their voices could be heard from the kitchen. As Jenny and the children started away from the table, the dispute moved into the dining room.

"You know that I nearly got supper on alone tonight," wailed Rachel, "and you promised me I could cut out that new dress I've been wanting to sew. Why do I have to help clean up again? When are you going to get some help! I can't do it all!"

"Well, I just didn't think we'd have so many folks staying over tonight," anguished Nellie. "I am tired too and I've got that whole kitchen of dishes to do by myself I suppose."

"I don't care," shouted Rachel, "I never get any time to myself. Just work, work, work all the time."

With a look of embarrassment, Nellie suddenly realized that Jenny was still in the room.

Gracious me, I thought everyone had left. Go on and work on your dress," said Nellie dejectedly, "I'll clean things up myself."

"Could I help you?" asked Jenny, "if you wouldn't mind. We slept all afternoon on the train. It would give me something to do. I can just keep an eye on the children at the same time."

"Well, sure," replied Nellie smiling. Well, sure, that would be real nice now. You kids can play right here in the dining room. There are some old picture books of Rachel's there on the little table in the corner. I keep it just for folks who stay over with children. There's a box there with some old toys in it too...help yourself....just don't go leaving them on the floor so's folks will step on them and fall down.

Robbie loved books, although he hardly ever saw one. He was in his glory as he guided his sisters to the little table and chairs and sat down.

Jenny, seeing they were taken care of, quickly begin to clear the large table and together, she and Nellie, soon had the dishes done, the breakfast table set and had made preparation for the morning meal.

You sure seem to know your way around the kitchen," stated Nellie, delighted at how much the two of them had accomplished. "Wish I could find help like that around here."

"As long as I can keep the children where I can watch them...I wouldn't mind helping until we can get a train out to St. Louis," said Jenny.

"It might be a couple of days," mulled Nellie. "I'd give you your room and board free, if you really want to work 'til your train leaves. Rachel loves kids—she could watch them some."

"All right," agreed Jenny, thinking that would certainly help her with her dwindling money problems.

"The children will be fine though," said Jenny, "they can just play there in the dining room where I can see them." She wasn't too sure about having Rachel baby–sit.

By the time Nellie and Jenny had finished, the children were ready to go to bed. They had enjoyed the books with Robbie even trying to read some to the girls. They were soon settled comfortably for the night with Robbie on the cot that Nellie had brought in and Jenny with the two girls. The bed was large and it gave them plenty of room.

Jenny rose early next morning, leaving the children to sleep and went down to the kitchen to get an early start. Over the next two days, she became acquainted with Rachel and found her to really be a responsible person. Rachel just didn't have much of a social life for a young person living at the boarding house as she did. Jenny even allowed Rachel to take the youngsters off her hands some, much to their delight, as Rachel proved to be really good with them. She told them stories and played with them on the big front porch.

After nearly a week went by, Jenny began to wonder if they would ever leave Sedalia. Finally, word came through by wire that most of the tracks were repaired and the trains could move again.

The first passenger train to St. Louis would be coming through about 7:30 the next morning. Nellie tried to convince Jenny to stay but Jenny immediately purchased tickets saying she had business in St. Louis that would not wait.

The weather seemed at long last to have really settled and the last four days had been dry with sunshine.

Jenny helped set up for breakfast and then hurried herself and the children off to bed so they would not be too tired for the morning trip.

Sometime in the night the moon rose with a silver light and gave an almost daylight appearance to everything. The vast canopy of the heavens was filled with a myriad of stars. A soft breeze stirred the curtains at the windows that had been left open.

The neighing of a horse woke Jenny. She stirred sleepily in the comfort of her soft pillow. The moon filled the room with an irradiate glow and the air was sweet and fresh. She raised up to look out of the window—was that a train coming in? The room was resplendent so bathed in moonlight. Jenny got out of bed and went to the window. The train was just slowing now. The station platform was directly across the street form her window. Oh, she thought, just a few more hours and we will be headed east. We'll stop just long enough in St. Louis to take care of the business with David's attorney and then...on to Boston! She hadn't told Nellie they were going to Boston, just in case Jacque was ever able to trace them and question her. Something seemed amiss across the street though. Several men on horseback had charged up to the train. Were they waiting for someone to arrive from the incoming train? Not likely at this hour. Something about them seemed familiar. Was she dreaming? No! She was wide awake now, peering into the night, the bright moonlight illuminating the objects below. She was sure these men looked familiar...Yes! Yes! She could see them very plainly now. They were Jacque's friends. They had come to the farm so many times in the past few months, but what were they doing here in Sedalia, meeting a train at this time of night?

Then another rider swiftly joined the others, barking out orders as several men jumped from their horses and boarded the train, which had now come to a standstill. Jenny recognized the man. It was Jacque.

Crack! Crack! Was that...Jenny put her hands over her ears. It sounded again and once more. The men were back on their horses now, leaving someone lying on the ground in front of the coach. The riders came galloping across the street and passed under Jenny's window. They did not see her.

People came running now, toward the fallen man and shouting, "Robbers! Robbers! Get some help! This man has been shot!"

Glancing toward the bed, she was relieved to see that the children had heard nothing. The noise hadn't disturbed them. Jenny didn't own a robe so she grabbed the spread off the bed and threw it over her shoulders and quickly went downstairs. Nellie was up as was almost everyone else in the house. Shouts from the engineer and others on the train had awakened most everyone near the station. The conductor had been shot and some of the men were carrying him to the doctor's office down the street.

"Oh, this is awful, just awful," lamented Nellie scurrying about while ringing her hands together, "never has such a thing happened here before. Oh, that poor, poor man."

"Is he alive?" asked Jenny.

"We don't know, won't know until Doc looks him over," answered the distressed Nellie.

People were now coming out on their porches, trying to see what had happened.

"Oh, my, don't go outside," warned Nellie to her guests. "Mr. Carter from next door, he runs the post office, you know, well, he's going up and down the street telling everybody to stay inside as we don't know where them robbers went. They may be gone, but maybe not. Somebody said that they had ridden right over their front porch. We could have all been murdered in our beds."

"I'm going to make some coffee for everyone," said Nellie in a still shaky but calmer voice. "Want to help me, Jenny?" she inquired.

"Alright," said Jenny "but let me check on the children first."

By the time Jenny rejoined the others, news had come that the conductor was seriously wounded, but was still alive.

Jenny took her coffee and sat down in the chair in the parlor where the others had gathered, each giving the other their version of what had happened.

What shall I do thought Jenny. I can't tell these people I knew those men. Perhaps they would even think that I was involved. I must get away from here. Oh, will morning ever come?

Why had she ever married Jacque? He was so good looking—with his dark eyes and black hair. Then, he was attentive and caring during the time of David's sudden death. A warm response that was most welcomed and which did help to fill the void she felt in her heart and lessen her grief. He had assured her that he was a fine Christian who loved her and the children and he seemed to demonstrate this by his thoughtfulness for her every need. So, soon she consented to marry him. He changed from almost the very first day after the wedding. Too late, she realized the trap in which she had become ensnared. It made no difference how hard Jenny tried to make a home for every-one—Jacque just grew worse and worse. She had no idea what he did in his prolonged unaccounted for absences, until now.

People were starting to drift off to their rooms.

"I hear they didn't get much," said one of the cattlemen. "That train was supposed to have the gold shipment, but due to all the flooding they shipped it south. Wasn't much of value on that train."

"Ya, too bad they had to shoot the conductor," stated the other man, "they're in for trouble now, especially if he doesn't make it."

Jenny couldn't take any more, she said goodnight to Nellie and went up to her room. No one had questioned her and she was relieved. She now wished to put all of this out of her mind. She wanted a chance for a better life for her and the children. Somewhere far from here where perhaps even her own nightmares would flee away from her forever.

"Come, morning, Please come?" she whispered, "come, morning, please, oh, please come.

Chapter Six

Jenny was dressed and packed before the children woke. They had no idea of what had transpired during the night. She awakened them for an early breakfast and after saying their good–byes and promising to someday return for a visit, they cheerfully boarded the long awaited train for St. Louis.

Nellie had packed them a plentiful basket of food—enough provisions to last a week—Jenny was sure.

Jenny had learned before leaving that the wounded conductor was much improved and was beginning to give some details of the robbery. However, none of the highwaymen had been apprehended.

Robbie and Elizabeth were so excited about going to St. Louis that they were hard to settle down. It didn't matter to Jacqueline, whatever made the rest of them happy, made her happy too.

Jenny looked fondly at the children as they laughed and talked excitedly together. Robbie with his light brown hair and earnest gray eyes looked so much like his father, although he often appeared somber in contrast to David's cheerful countenance.

Elizabeth was almost as tall as Robbie, even though he was nearly a year older than she. Even at her young age, she was a devoted companion to her brother. Sometimes Jenny thought they spoke sentences together. Robbie would start a sentence and Elizabeth would finish it. His thoughts were profound and intent, but Elizabeth seemed to catch whatever pulsed through his mind. While he was beginning to speak. Elizabeth would pick–up and finish what he wanted to say. How she loved her dear brother, even though she was often a tease. Even in time of great turmoil she made them all laugh with her playful wit.

Elizabeth and Jacqueline were a contrast in appearance. Elizabeth had auburn hair and green eyes like her mother, while Jacqueline had been graced with blonde curls and blue eyes, as David said, "a copy of his mother."

Robbie and Elizabeth loved Jacqueline with all their hearts. At times Jenny felt they were overly protective of her, but with Jacque around it was easy to understand why.

Robbie and Elizabeth now begin to question Jenny about what it was like when they lived in St. Louis. She attempted to explain as much as she could. Robbie said that he wanted to see the place they had lived, but Jenny explained they would try and come back to visit at a later time. When it was safer, she thought, for she was constantly aware of the need to put distance between them and Jacque. St. Louis was also home to Jacque; at least he had spent a lot of time in that vicinity. She did not want to encounter him or his evil companions, but hoped they were keeping a low profile at this time. Still, no one seemed to have any knowledge of who robbed the train so they could without too much fear openly be seen anywhere.

Upon their arrival in the city, Jenny was relieved to find places of business still open. She thanked the Lord that it was only a short walk to the bank from the station.

In no time at all, she found the attorneys office on the second floor of the bank building. Upon entering she gave a girl at the desk her name and was told there would be a short wait and to please be seated. After some time they were ushered into an inner office that read 'Joseph J. Barton' on the door.

"Well, hello, Mrs. Boshart," greeted the gentleman as he came around the desk and offered his hand in a friendly shake.

"I hardly expected to see you so soon," he stated, "I do hope you are feeling much better." He looked toward the door as if anticipating someone else to join them.

"I came as quickly as I could," she replied, rather surprised at his statement. "The flooding has made it difficult to travel," she added.

"Yes, that is true," he agreed with a puzzled look on his face. "That is why I am quite amazed that you have arrived so quickly.

"We came on a train," offered Elizabeth, "they move really fast," she assured him with a big smile.

"Elizabeth be quiet," whispered Robbie grabbing the little girls' hand.

The attorney laughed and offered them chairs asking them to make themselves comfortable. Finally, he went around and sat down behind the desk producing some legal papers that he offered to her to read and sign.

"You understand, Mrs. Boshart," he offered, "that because the insurance company was unable to find you, the matter was turned over to us. It is necessary that we verify your signature on these documents so I am pleased that I had met you sometime ago and can vouch that you are indeed the Mrs. Boshart mentioned in these documents."

Jenny had forgotten that David had brought an attorney to the house about the business on one occasion and she had signed some papers. It had completely slipped her mind.

"I'm sorry," replied Jenny, "I didn't remember you."

"Well, it was sometime ago and much has happened since then," he answered, "but, it would be very hard to forget you Mrs. Boshart, especially with your red hair." Then feeling he might be misunderstood he went on to give her the particulars of her claim.

Jenny silently gave praise to God when it was revealed to her the amount of the policy. It wasn't a fortune, but it was far more than she had dared to hope for.

Finally, the business she came to pursue was finished and Jenny rose to leave. The attorney shook her hand again.

"I am surprised that your husband didn't make it clear when he was here yesterday, that you were already en route," he declared. "Mr. Boshart seemed a little upset when I told him you had to personally sign the papers. It was then that he stated that you were very ill. Please give him my greetings and I am sure that he will be pleased that this business has been concluded."

"So Jacque has been here," she whispered to herself as they left the bank building. "He had no right to that money—no right at all." Then she in the next breath thanked God for his watching over her and what rightfully belonged to her and the children.

Jacque could be anywhere; he could be watching them now. Well, there was little she could do about it and she had to return to the train station. Once there she purchased tickets to Boston, Massachusetts. It all seemed so unreal, as suddenly, she had ample finances to care for herself and the children. Even with the threat of Jacque's appearing, she felt free.

Upon finding that the trip to Boston did not leave until early evening, Jenny decided on a surprise for the children. It wasn't easy for her to travel from the station to the shops, aware that Jacque might greet them anywhere along the way. Still, she could encounter his presence just as easily in the train terminal and she and the children desperately needed new attire. Their shabby appearance was a sad reminder of all they had endured and it would certainly give her self–confidence a boost if they were more suitably dressed.

Entering a shop with ready–made clothes in the window, no time for tailor made articles, Jenny soon selected two new dresses for each of the girls. The she purchased a suit with an extra pair of trousers, a shirt, and a tie for Robbie. She selected two cool summer frocks for herself, one a pale green with a wide white–laced collar which enhanced the red of her hair. The other had a background of white with small lavender flowers in a delicately embroidered pattern. She then purchased wide–brimmed bonnets trimmed with satin ribbons for her and the girls. Finally, new shoes for all. Oh, she felt light and free. As they left the shop, she had to look down at her feet to see if they really touched the sidewalk. Were those her feet? Gone were the worn–out work shoes.

She had chosen to wear the white dress. It made her feel almost like a child again. As long as she could remember, she had loved white. Somehow, white made her happy most of the time. Soft–billowing, white–like clouds floating placidly in the blue sky.

She glanced down at the two little girls and Robbie. How fine they all looked. Others were in agreement silently, as they cast admiring glances at the little family as they made their way back to the station.

Just before they arrived at the depot, they passed a small toy–shop Jenny could not resist investigating. She first checked the big clock on the street corner... yes, they still had time. Inside was a dream world of toys of every kind. Finally, with some persuasion she encouraged them each to choose some small and inexpensive item. They must hurry now.

Robbie chose a handsome book with pictures of sailing vessels and stories of faraway places that he had never even heard of. Elizabeth couldn't choose, but settled for a small, children's dresser set, with hand mirror, brush and comb. Jacqueline had fallen in love with a soft stuffed rag doll. It made crying sounds when you flipped its face down. She cooed lovingly to it as she cradled it in her arms. The prices were more than she wanted to pay, but she felt she was celebrating all those Christmases and birthdays they had missed.

So it was when they stepped onto the train heading for Boston, their demeanor changed. Jenny had always carried herself with dignity and had a natural grace that even under great affliction still quickly surfaced at the slightest release of distress. As a child, she had never known much happiness, but had always felt that somehow, sometime, something would cause the heaviness and desolation to dissolve.

David had penetrated that engulfment of gloom. He had given her a reason for which to live. When she had married David, she felt she had been lifted from the abyss of despair. Had David lived she was sure her life would have been fulfilled. He had led her to Christ, and this precious relation-ship would never be forsaken. Then, there were her cherished babies, each one was woven into her heart with twines of golden love forevermore.

Today as she stepped light–footed along the aisle of the train, gently prodding the children into their seats, Jenny felt her spirit soar to a height she had never known before. She was free! She wanted to shout. She wanted to sing. She wanted to laugh. Instead, she seated herself quietly with the children and smoothed the soft white skirt of her dress...softly...something touching...floating....white—what was it? Don't leave thought...Oh, Oh, it always goes...my head...Oh, don't ache today. Please go away...black thoughts...I will be happy. The train was now in motion and they were on their way.

She was oblivious of the squinted–eyed man who took a seat far in the rear of the car, nor did she notice the interest he paid the conductor when the tickets were collected.

As the train puffed its way through the countryside and rolled in and out of towns and villages, Jenny begin to realize they had successfully made their escape and were safe from the perils they had left behind. It had been nearly ten days now since they had left the remote dreary farm. It had been a long and precarious journey but Jacque had not found them.

The long ride on the passenger train was very tranquil with people all around them, some getting on, others leaving at their appointed destined stops. As they rode on through the night and slept comfortably with soft pillows, provided by the porter, they were not alone. Jenny didn't think she ever wanted to be alone again.

She had been such a lonely child and the desolate farm had been almost too much for her. It was her strong faith in God and her great love for her children that had given her the courage to continue on. Some days it was all she could do to physically push her weary self through her many daily chores. She didn't know what the future held or even if they had a future, but she kept clinging faithfully to the scripture—Romans 8:28, "and we know that all things work together for good to them that love God, to them who are called according to his purpose." She had hoped that Jacque would change, and to this purpose, she had prayed; but it seemed that Jacque had purposed in his heart to do evil and evil he did. She knew that God had now lead them out and away from what she was sure would have ended in a calamity. Most likely their untimely demise. She knew she could not have survived many more of Jacque's beatings. She had began to wonder honestly about her sanity. The nightmares, she had always had them, but they had grown so much worse, that lately she had awakened in the dark farmhouse at night screaming out in terror, unable to catch her breath.

In the short time she and David had been married, Jenny had almost conquered her fear of her intimidating dreams. He was so comforting, so consoling. Jenny could not comprehend why God had chosen to call David home so young. Yet, she knew someday she would meet David again. Yes, he would be waiting for her, with that big contagious smile on his face that lit up your heart. As long as she was able, she would tenderly care for, protect, and provide for their children.

She prayed that Jacque would never find them unless he changed. However, if he did she would handle that when the time came. At least they would not be alone and at his mercy in the wild, foreboding, and dark woods again. Never! Never! She thought, with a shudder of apprehension.

Chapter Seven

They had reached their destination. The miles and miles of countryside and towns along the way had sped past without the slightest thought of weariness or complaining on Jenny's or the children's part. No, quite the contrary, it had been an adventure to them made even more interesting with the anticipation of a new life in a new environment.

"Oh, the air!" exclaimed Jenny as she took long breaths of fresh, salty breezes that wafted its way inland from the sea.

The ocean can't be far away," she told Robbie, "and we are going to watch great ships come and go from the harbor whenever we like." How the thought exhilarated her.

With a smile of sudden joy, she lifted Jacqueline up and hugged her tight as she twirled around in a circle. Elizabeth caught up in the excitement of the moment begin to jump about as she attempted to mimic her mother's graceful pirouette. Instead of displaying grace, she spun out of control into the crowd and violently collided with the pudgy figure of the itinerant salesman from Sedalia. His luggage went flying and he fell with a heavy jolt to the platform. The contents of his bag was ejected from the case revealing a small pistol as it lay there for an instant gleaming in the sunlight. Seemingly, unruffled and unhurt, the man scampered to his feet, secured his luggage, and disappeared in the throng of people.

"Oh, dear. Oh, dear," wailed Elizabeth as Robbie pulled her upright from the crumpled position where she had landed.

"Elizabeth, you silly clown," admonished Robbie as he tried to determine if she was really hurt.

"He...He...knocked...all...all...my breth out, I think," said the child, but her green eyes still danced with mischief.

Jenny stood staring after the strange little man. Something about him had made her feel uneasy at the boarding house. His staring at them with his squinty little eyes was unnerving but presuming it was because of his poor vision she thought no more about it.

"Elizabeth," said Jenny as they collected their belongings and left the platform. "You certainly owe that man an apology, but he's gone now. I am not sure if Boston is ready for you, young lady." That question might become more pertinent in the years to come. Elizabeth shrugged it off with a giggle.

Finally, after asking directions and with some searching they were able to locate a suitable hotel. The room was small and three flights up but it was inexpensive and it would do for now.

Leaving what belongings they had at the hotel, they set out to explore the city

"Wow!" shouted Robbie, "I never saw so many people in all my life!"

"I think maybe everyone in the whole world lives here," explained Elizabeth with delight.

"Sometimes you are so ridiculous, Elizabeth. You know that there are lots of people living in other places," retorted Robbie shaking his head in disbelief.

"That's probable because they visit other places but everyone lives here," she stated with a smug look of authority. Elizabeth never considered herself to be wrong about anything.

"Think what you want," said Robbie as he was now too caught up in the awe of the city unfolding before his eyes to argue any further with his sister.

There were horse drawn carriages, carts and drays, buggies, wagons and trolleys crowding the streets. Throngs and multitudes of people were moving in every direction along the streets and sidewalks. Venders, clerks, shoppers, common laborers, those with business appointments to keep, some coming from others going to places of business or interest, some hurrying and others strolling casually taking in the sights before them.

So many interesting buildings mused Jenny as she became enraptured with the scene before her. Oh, so many different kinds of decorative architecture. There were tall buildings, erect and reaching up into the sky, others not as tall but ornamental with sculptured columns and concrete designs. Some had balconies with awnings on the street level. There were multi–windowed hotels, stately buildings as if a bank or house of business, all tightly abutted together. Although each seemed to be distinct and unique, yet they blended together in a line of one congruous mass of structural beauty reaching out as far as the eye could see.

After sometime they came upon a marketplace. Holding a large display of vegetables was a child's wagon with a wooden rack. It wasn't new but appeared to be in considerably good condition.

"Could I help you with something?" asked the merchant. "These are good, fresh vegetables just picked yesterday," he continued.

It took a few minutes of friendly bartering, but soon the wagon was theirs. Elizabeth and Jacqueline blissfully climbed aboard. Walking became much more enjoyable for Robbie and Jenny.

They had arrived early in the day and rested so much during their train ride, that Jenny was now eager to survey the surrounding territory. What she was looking for she didn't exactly know, but, one thing for sure, she already loved Boston and meant to stay.

Having made some lunch purchases from the market where they had bought the wagon, they had a late lunch in the park along the way.

The park was small but overflowing with people. Businessmen attired in suits were sitting on benches reading their newspapers. Children some accompanied by their nanny, played on the green lawn. The sun was warm and the air fresh.

Jenny gave the children time to play. As she watched them, she was suddenly overcome with a sense of forlornness. Why had she come to a strange place she did not know? What had she accomplished by pursuing her vague and probably unrealistic dreams? What was it that had so compelled her to come? She so desired to provide her children with a good and proper home, but how was she to accomplish her goal?

Freeing herself from the dilemma, she blurted out, "Well! Sitting in an unfamiliar place and feeling sorry for myself is not going to bring about any good results." She decided it was time to go.

"Robbie…Elizabeth…Jacqueline," she called to the children. We are leaving now."

"Aw, we were just having fun," sputtered Robbie. Do we have to go now?"

The boy rarely gave Jenny a difficult time over anything, but he had made a friend, another boy he had met in the park. They had been tossing a ball back and forth to each other when Jenny called.

"I think we should leave, children. We have a long walk back to the hotel," Jenny explained.

"All right. Maybe I'll see you again," shouted Robbie to his new friend as they took their leave of each other.

Jenny thought she would take a shorter way back and cut down a side street across from the park. About two blocks along Jenny saw something that really caught her interest. It was a two–story, rather narrow, building in–between the larger structures on the block. It was detached on either side from the other buildings with a small courtyard on one side and a narrow walk on the other. The courtyard was enclosed with a black iron fence and the walk on the other side was enclosed with an iron–gate. It was a bustling area with lots of people on the street. There was a large front window and a door facing the street. The upper half of the door was glass and posted with a "for lease" sign. Even though the window was partially covered, Jenny could see there was a spacious room inside with what looked like a display counter of some kind. Jenny lifted the latch of the gate– it wasn't locked. Well, no harm in looking thought Jenny as she swung open the gate.

"Come," she said to Robbie pulling the two little girls in the wagon.

They went along the walk to a small, enclosed back yard, passing a side door along the way. The yard was small but had green grass and a single shade tree. The sunlight filtering down around the buildings made it all seem quite lovely. There was also a back door with a small roofed porch.

As they stood there looking around, Jenny heard the gate squeak and the sound of someone coming down the walk.

"Hello! Somebody back here," sounded a friendly voice from the front of the house.

"Yes, I do hope you will forgive us," Jenny answered as a man came around the corner of the building. "The gate wasn't locked and the sign said, 'for lease', we didn't mean to trespass."

"Well, now, what have we here," he asked placing his hands on his hips and looking pleasantly surprised.

He was of medium height, burly build, thinning hair, and a jolly ruddy appearance. Jenny liked him immediately.

"Well, I say now, what fine looking little ones and you don't need to be apologizing. Like the sign says, the place is for lease," he affirmed. "If you don't mind me takin' you through without my missus, I can show you the place now. She was comin' with me, but we had company just as we were going out the door.

"My name is Brown, but everyone around here calls me 'Brownie'," he said with a smile.

"My name is Jenny, Jenny Boshart and this is Robbie and in the wagon is Elizabeth and Jacqueline," said Jenny introducing herself and the children to Mr. Brown. "I guess it would be all right if you have time to show us," said Jenny, feeling that Mr. Brown was a gentleman.

"I just come over every couple days to check on the place," he explained, "It's been empty for about a year now. The building belonged to my wife's uncle. He taught music in the front part and lived in the back. He had a family back in the old country—went home to visit—the poor man took sick and died over there. Most all his furnishing are still here. My wife took what was personal. He just left everything to her.

As he was talking, he unlocked the back door and ush-ered them into a large comfortable kitchen. It had two windows overlooking the back yard, a cast–iron cook stove, table and chairs and plenty of cupboards within a small walk–in pantry. There was a door from the kitchen into a hallway and one at the other end that opened into a spacious front room where the uncle had taught music lessons. Brownie said he had moved the piano from the front room into the parlor, leaving only the huge counter in the, otherwise empty room. A door beside the built-in counter led to a hallway with a stairway leading upstairs. In front of the stairway was a locked door leading out to an unused courtyard. The three rooms upstairs had not been used for some time and Brownie didn't bother showing them. The hallway lead to double doors leading into the parlor, but they were closed and locked also. He then took them back along the short hallway into the kitchen again and from there directly into the parlor.

Jenny fell in love with the parlor. It hadn't downed on her that in the middle of the city would be such a quaint place—so homey and convenient. The parlor was a good size with windows facing on the courtyard. It was colorful. The rug that covered the floor was in a flowered pattern of a mixture of win and burgundy accented with deep greens. There was a couch with bulky pillows, two chairs and an old roll-top desk, a couple of small tables with oil lamps and some knickknacks. Heavy drapes hung framing the windows with sheers in between. An enormous piano against one wall, with a violin case lying on top, was covered with pages of music manuscripts.

To the left of the parlor was another small hallway on the right of that a bedroom with an immense bed and dresser. Straight ahead and down the hall a washroom and on the left of the hall, directly across from the bedroom, a unique tiny room with two walls of bookshelves filled with books from the floor to almost the ceiling. A small couch was sitting against one wall.

"That's it," said Brownie. "Were you thinking of using the place for business or maybe just for living here?" he asked.

"Well, both," answered Jenny. "The location seems really good and the living quarters so pleasant. Yes, I really do think it would be quite perfect for our needs.

"What kind of business do you have?" inquired Brownie.

"I would like to start a bakery," she answered, "I didn't see any close by."

"No, I don't believe there are any, at least not in this vicinity," replied Brownie.

"Are there any schools near by?" inquired Jenny.

"Yes, not more than two blocks away there is a private boys school, " said Brownie "and I think there are a couple more public schools not far from here."

"I do like it," said Jenny thoughtfully, "but, it is so large and I am not sure if we can afford it."

"Will the mister be joining you?" quizzed Brownie.

"No," said Jenny, "It's just the children and myself."

"I see," he answered. He liked Jenny with her quiet way and the children were well behaved. He had a feeling that Niki, his wife, would feel the same about them. So the price he quoted for leasing the place was much lower than he and Niki had agreed on previously. He felt they might not be able to afford too much.

Jenny couldn't believe the reasonable price he offered and before Brownie could change his mind, she quickly paid him two months rent in advance.

After explaining a little more about the gas lighting and the heat, Brownie left for home. He gave her the keys and informed her that Niki and he would be around in a couple of days to check on them and to bring the keys for the front door that he did not bring with him.

After the back door closed and he was gone, Jenny stood in amazement at her surrounding. It was perfect. With what cash she had left, she was sure she could afford to purchase supplies and begin her business within the week. How she wished they could stay the night and not go back to the hotel, but she had already paid for their nights' lodging and needed to pick up what few things they had left in the hotel room.

It was getting late and she wasn't quite sure how far they had walked from the hotel so even though they did not want to leave, Jenny felt they should start back. Evening was coming soon and with it the dark. The city seemed so friendly in the daylight, but she wasn't sure about the night.

The children were so excited. They had gone from room to room trying out the well–padded comfortable couch and chairs, and even softly touching the piano keys. Robbie couldn't believe all the books.

"What are they about, Mama?" he asked Jenny.

"Oh, all kinds of things," she answered, "history, religion, music, even Latin," she continued as she ran her hand across the rows of books. "But, remember," she cautioned, they are not our books and we must be very careful with them.

"I will, I will be so careful," Robbie answered his mother, and Elizabeth and Jacqueline. "I don't think you should look at them unless Mama and I help you," he added, looking very grown–up.

Elizabeth smiled with an understanding smile. She was sure she could handle anything as well as Robbie could, but she would keep it to herself.

The kitchen was stocked with pots and pans and dishes. Jenny felt that even though the former owner had been a music teacher, he must also have liked to cook. Just about every utensil she would need to bake was housed in the cupboards.

Finally, Jenny encouraged all three children to ride in the wagon and although it was a little crowded it would be faster.

As she locked the back door, church bells were chiming in the distance and birds were beginning to sing their evening songs and Jenny's heart was happy again.

It was farther than Jenny had thought. They had really walked a considerable distance and it was dark before they arrived back at the hotel.

In the morning, Jenny decided it was a good idea to have breakfast at the hotel, as they had gone directly to bed the night before, all being too tired to eat. She could then stop at the market and order the supplies she needed on the way to their new home.

Breakfast over, Jenny put Jacqueline and Elizabeth and their old satchel in the wagon. Robbie chose to walk.

It was a gray and overcast morning in total contrast to yesterday's lovely weather. It had apparently rained hard in the night and there was a wet, foggy mist in the air. Jenny liked it. It was cool and refreshed her tired mind. There was a faint smell of fish in the air, something about it all stirred Jenny's thoughts to faint memories she could not connect together. She didn't have time to dwell on them. She wanted to get to the market now.

Soon after, they left the hotel it begin to drizzle rain. Well, no matter it felt good, besides it wasn't cold—not really. The air had a much different quality than the heavy humid air they were accustomed to. The streets were very wet from last nights' rain.

Traffic was heavy in spite of the wet weather and as they started to cross a busy street, a horse and carriage came hurrying around the corner splashing them from head to foot with muddy water.

"You, simpleton!" screamed Jenny at the fast disappearing carriage. Her face was so covered with muddy water she could barely see. She wiped at her eyes with her hand but it made them sting and smart from the particles of embedded dirt. She felt her hair tumble unto her shoulders so drenched with the muddy mess that the pins were sliding out and falling to the wet pavement. Her shoes sloshed with water as she moved to help Robbie. He was in the same predicament as she was. The girls it seemed had been spared from the brunt of the deluge.

Jenny was so upset that she failed to recognize that a young gentleman had alighted from his carriage and was now offering her his handkerchief. In her agitated state, she almost waved it away. He was uncertain as what he could do to calm her.

"I saw that carriage nearly run over you and was really alarmed. What can I do to help you?" he asked, feeling inept to cope with the situation but still holding out the handkerchief as a means of assistance.

Jenny reached and took it, dabbing at her muddied face.

"Are you hurt anywhere?" he questioned nervously.

"No...no, I think we are all right. Just very wet and muddy," answered Jenny from behind the mask of mud covering her face.

"I am afraid your handkerchief is ruined," she added.

"Don't worry about it. Could I give you a ride somewhere?" he questioned. He was rather mystified as to why the young lady was out in the rain, pulling the children in a wagon. However, he felt it was not his business to ask.

"My name is Benjamin Forbes, Ben to my friends. I am a practicing attorney, well, that is, I am a lawyer who had just hung out his shingle yesterday, so I haven't any practice yet," he grinned.

"It is beginning to rain hard and you are all very wet, I assure you that I have only your and the children's welfare in mind when I offer you my carriage." He said as he smiled pleasantly again. Could I take you somewhere? Anywhere out of this weather?"

The rain was now coming down in torrents and Jenny decided to trust their lives to this young gentleman. She looked at the comical expression on his face as he tried not to show any amusement at her appearance.

"I certainly would not accept your hospitality," mumbled Jenny, "but we are in a bit of a predicament."

Ben gave a sigh of relief and lifted the children into the covered carriage. He helped Jenny up and grabbed up the little wagon. By this time, he was quite wet himself.

"Now, where would you like to go?" he asked looking quizzically at Jenny.

Jenny suddenly realized with a look of consternation on her face that she did not know the street number or the name of the street. She usually was so precise in all that she did. She knew how to get there, but in her excitement about finding the place, she had not thought about the address.

"I don't know the name of the street," she answered softly feeling quite embarrassed.

Robbie spoke up and quickly added, "We can show you where we want to go."

"Yes," said Jenny, "we only found the place yesterday and I quite forgot to get the address."

"I see," responded Ben, but he couldn't hold back a small chuckle. "I am sorry," he continued after trying to stifle his laughter, "but you do look a little, oh, let's say different."

Jenny's red tresses had completely fallen down and her dress was covered with mud. It was hard to have any look of dignity about her at all and now a perfect stranger was laughing at her. She stole a disgruntled look at the gentleman beside her. He was rather good looking kind of a long nose and rather slender face. Gray eyes amusingly looking at her, an amiable smile and also because of his graciousness toward her, very wet.

Suddenly, the whole situation seemed ridiculously humorous to her. She smiled at him in relief that such a considerate gentleman happened by to assist her in her plight.

"I guess we are a sorry sight," she said. "You're very kind and brave to help us and give us a ride."

"Well, let's find this place," he replied.

In the downpour, it was difficult to give instructions as to the proper street and when to turn, but after a few mistakes and goodhearted joking, they finally found the place.

Benjamin insisted on carrying the little wagon and satchel for them and made sure they were safely inside before he took his leave.

As Ben closed the door and walked back to his carriage, he silently hoped that would not be his last encounter with the intriguing red–haired lady and family. He had somehow enjoyed their brief but unusual adventure. She was very different from anyone he had ever met before. She certainly made a grand but impressive entrance into his life he thought as he reflected on the recent events of this morning. He wondered where her husband was and why he wasn't with them.

Chapter Eight

It took Robbie and Jenny longer to remove the mud from themselves and their clothing than it did to put away the contents of the satchel in which they had carried their clothing. Finally, the children were busy acquainting themselves with everything. Jenny started going through the cupboards and pantry, straightening and taking inventory so to speak, as to what she would need to start her business. She had been cleaning and taking stock for sometime when a knock sounded at the back door. Brownie had brought his wife around to meet the new tenets. She was about Jenny's height, a little over weight, slightly graying hair, but nicely attired.

"This is Mrs. Brown," he started to say, but his wife didn't let him finish.

"My name is Niki," she said with a friendly smile, "and Brownie tells me your name is Janie?"

"No," smiled Jenny. "My name is Jenny."

"Well, that was real good for Brownie to get it that close," laughed Niki. "He never remembers names. However, he hasn't talked about anything much else but the children and you since he came home yesterday and told me he had rented the place. You sure made a good impression on him.

Brownie was looking most embarrassed at his wife's comments and his weathered face was showing a little flush.

"Oh, now don't you go getting upset Brownie," Niki teased, "But you sure didn't tell me how pretty she is."

Before anyone could comment further, Robbie and Elizabeth came into the kitchen to see who their guests were.

"So, these are the children. Oh, Brownie, look at that gorgeous red hair!" exclaimed Niki, "and skin like peaches and cream. What is your name, honey?" she asked Elizabeth.

"Elizabeth," she answered.

"And your are? Oh, what is your name?" inquired Niki.

"My name is Robert," stated the boy.

"What beautiful children," said Niki, "And Elizabeth you look just like your mother."

"I look like Robbie too," replied Elizabeth.

"Well, that is true. You do favor him some, but you didn't get the red hair, did you son," remarked Niki.

"Mama says I look just like my dad who has gone to heaven," answered Robbie.

"Oh, the children's father has passed away then, how sad," said Niki.

"I thought you told me that there were three little ones, Brownie?" asked Niki looking at him questioningly.

"There are," interrupted Jenny, "but we had a quick lunch and she is now sleeping on the big bed.

"How old are they?" asked Niki.

"Robbie is seven. Elizabeth is six and Jacqueline is three," explained Jenny.

"I understand you want to start a bakery, is that right?" asked Niki.

"Yes," replied Jenny, "if all goes well and there are no real problems. I believe I could start by the first of the week.

"That's kind of why we came over for today. Brownie thought you were planning on moving in today and we wanted to bring you the key to the front door. We've kept the place up as best we could, but it really isn't something we wanted to take on. Brownie owns a couple of fishing trawlers and we have a comfortable house down close to the wharf. We try to get up her every day or so to check on things, but it keeps us going. It is a relief to have it rented," explained Niki.

By this time, Brownie had wandered off into the parlor at the urging of the two children. He was now explaining what little he knew about the piano in answer to their curiosity.

Robbie was so fascinated with the violin on top of the piano that Brownie took it from the case and placed it in the boy's hands. Robbie had never seen anything like it before in his life. Brownie showed him how the uncle used to hold it and placed the bow in his hand. The child ran his fingers up and down the strings as he wondered what sound it would make. Oh, how he wished he might make it play.

When Niki and Jenny followed them into the room, Robbie was drawing the bow across the stings producing shrill, squeaking sounds.

"Robbie!" exclaimed Jenny startling the child, "please be careful. That looks like an expensive violin." She really didn't know anything about it but knew she did not want Robbie to harm it in any way.

"It would really be good if the children could take some lessons," said Brownie. "They seem so interested and it would make good use of the instruments."

"Well, if they really want to," added Niki, "Professor Grant, uncles friend is just a short distance away. He teaches in the school during the school term also."

"Oh, Mama," chimed in Robbie, "could we possibly take lessons?"

"We'll see," replied Jenny with an enthusiastic look. "Perhaps when school begins. Right now, I must put all my attention on starting the bakery.

"What do you need to do first?" asked Niki. "The trawlers are in for a few days for needed repairs so Brownie was wondering what he could do to help. Have you looked over the room yet where you plan to sell your goods?"

"No, I was kind of taking inventory of the kitchen and pantry" said Jenny as she thoughtfully surveyed the room and its possibilities. "I am really amazed at all this cooking equipment just sitting around waiting to be used."

"Uncle liked to cook," replied Niki. "He never married and I think it relaxed him to bake or cook up something special. He had a lot of friends and he entertained often. Music was his first love, but cooking was a close second.

"I brought along my tool box in case you needed any help," interjected Brownie shyly, not wanting to seem too obtrusive. If you would give me some idea of what you were planning on doing to the front room, I'd be glad to begin work."

"To be perfectly honest with you both," said Jenny softly, I feel the rent was extremely low and I couldn't let you do any more."

"Nonsense," argued Niki, "we have been trying to rent this place for a year now and we want to help you get it ship–shape for your business. After all, if you're a success, then we get our rent," she laughed, and turning to Brownie continued, "Right, Brownie?"

Brownie had already headed for the front room. By late in the afternoon, Jenny and Niki had cleaned the kitchen and pantry spotlessly and when Jacqueline awoke the two women and little girls made a trip to the market. The sun had come out brightly and was fast drying up all the wetness.

Jenny ordered flour and sugars, lard and other cooking items, supplies that would be delivered the next morning. Then she purchased staples for their own nourishing necessities. While Brownie and Robbie worked together in the front of the house, cleaning walls, washing windows and mopping floors, Jenny and Niki prepared supper. Niki was amazed at Jenny's deftness in the kitchen.

"Jenny," said Niki in disbelief after working with her a short while, "I have never seen anyone prepare food as you do. Where did you learn all of this? I am really astonished. Your bakery should be a complete success. You are no ordinary cook, young lady."

"I grew up around people who were good cooks. I was trained by one of the best chefs in the country," explained Jenny. "It was just a part of my life. I guess I took to it naturally."

Niki had found a tablecloth and napkins folded away in a kitchen drawer and soon they all were sitting down at the table to a splendid meal. Even the table was well set.

So much had been accomplished, and a warm friendship had developed between the two families, one that throughout the coming years would only broaden and grow stronger.

The music room had now become a bakery. The counter wiped clean and all the glass shining. Brownie had gone upstairs and found two little tables, which he carried down stairs and set up with an assortment of straight backed chairs, where patrons could be seated while they enjoyed tea and cookies.

Jenny had decided to open the bakery on Monday. This being mid–week Brownie said he would like to make a sign for the front of the building.

"I don't know when I have seen Brownie so contented," said Niki as she and Jenny cleared away the dinner dishes. Brownie had retired to the parlor with Jacqueline seated on his lap with Elizabeth and Robbie positioned close by attentively engrossed by tales of the sea so vividly portrayed for their young imaginative minds to ponder.

"Brownie loves children and so do I," explained Niki as she watched Brownie and the children together. "We had one, a little boy—he died of Diphtheria when he was two. It's been really hard for both of us. It was a long time ago—I guess that's why we enjoy so much other peoples' children when they will let us. Well, it's been a good afternoon—sure hope we haven't been meddlesome. Brownie should be back on the boat in a few more days so we won't be so much in your way."

"Niki," said Jenny warmly, placing her hand on her shoulder, "you have both been so kind and helpful today. I could never have accomplished all of this without your help."

"The children really need some one like Brownie in their lives," added Jenny. "Let's just hope they don't wear him out completely tonight," laughed Jenny looking toward the parlor.

"Yes, it must be hard with their father gone," sighed Niki compassionately.

Jenny looked at Niki as if gathering her thoughts and after a few moments feeling obligated to reveal all to her dear friends began to explain.

"Niki, I feel I must be perfectly honest with you," said Jenny discerning the loyalty of this gracious lady. "My first husband the children's father was a fine man and he went home to be with the Lord, but my second husband, is alive. That is the reason we are here in Boston, as far from him as we could remove ourselves. If he ever finds us, it would be disastrous for the children and myself. I can't tell you any more just now, but I felt I owed you and Brownie the truth. However, I must ask you to please not repeat this to anyone, our lives may be in great danger if you do."

"I won't even speak of it to Brownie if you would rather I didn't," reasoned Niki with a look of apprehension for Jenny and the children.

"No, I think he should know, but never mention it to anyone else, please," asked Jenny.

No more was spoken on the subject and when Niki and Brownie finally left to catch the trolley home, it was with plans having been made to meet at the house on Sunday morning so that they could all attend Sunday services together.

With the children sleeping, Robbie in the little alcove room on the comfortable couch and the two little girls in the big bed in the room across the hall, Jenny collapsed into a soft chair in the parlor. She was very tired, but happy. It was so good to have friends. She had so few. Perhaps she could start a new life here. Even if she never found her mothers' family or discovered her real identity, Jenny was glad she had come to this place. She felt such peace. No one here to terrorize her or the children, or degrade her with intimidating humiliation. For the first time in years, she could think clearly and feel really free.

"Thank you, Lord. Thank you," she breathed prayerfully as she fell asleep snuggled down into the comfortable chair.

Instead of the dark nightmares, she dreamed of soft voices and veiled faces as fragments of a childish prayer drifted through the hallways of her mind. She slumbered on through the night, home at last—home at last.

Chapter Nine

On Friday, Brownie and Niki rapped lightly on the back door, after greeting the children at play in the yard.

"Yoohoo," yelled Niki, "I just stopped by to see how everything is going."

The kitchen was filled with the aroma of baked goods. There were fresh baked cookies of several different kinds and warm loaves of bread sitting on the sideboard of the cupboard fresh from the oven.

"Well, Hello," answered Jenny cheerfully as she stepped from the front hallway.

"I was preparing the shelves in the front counter for my baked goods."

"It sure looks and smells mighty good," stated Brownie rubbing his paunch of a stomach.

"This is just a little practice work," replied Jenny. "Help yourself. There is a pot of coffee on the stove. Here let me get some cups and saucers and see what you think."

Brownie didn't need to be coaxed. He let Jenny pour him a cup of freshly brewed coffee and soon was eagerly satisfying his sweet tooth. Niki didn't mind helping herself either. Jenny joined them and listened good–naturedly as the two praised her baking abilities.

"You know, Jenny," said Brownie after putting away at least half a dozen or so cookies. You've got a winner here. There is no doubt in this old seafarers mind that your problem will be keeping up with the demand."

Jenny sat sipping her coffee contentedly listening to the kind compliments of her new friends. She felt her confidence has just risen to a new high. She thought back to how Jacque had never ceased to demean her. It didn't matter what she endeavored to do, nothing was good enough. Jenny herself wasn't any good. The second day of their marriage, he slapped her and told her she was trash. He called her the daughter of a prostitute and said she had no father. Furthermore, she was to be grateful that he had married her and whatever he told her to do from then on, she was to obey him explicitly. He was the head of the house. David, by contrast, had never spoken to her or treated her like that. As a child, she had no feeling of self worth, and after a while, she just begin to accept and believe what Jacque told her was true. What he did to her seemed so unimportant, but what he failed to understand was Jenny's sense of protection for her children. The day Jacque attacked Robbie was the day Jenny began to come alive.

"Jenny," said Niki, "I've been thinking—isn't it going to be rather difficult to do all the baking, run the store, and watch the children all at the same time?"

"Oh, I don't think so," replied Jenny. "The children are so good and mind me so well, and most of the baking I do in the very early morning hours so by the time the selling part of the bakery begins I will be finished in the kitchen. I thought I would open the double doors in the front hallway leading to the parlor, that way I can observe what is going on with the children."

"Well, just in case you should need help," said Niki, "I know of a kindly older woman who attends our church. You will probably meet her Sunday. Actually, I was kind of hoping you might need help. This lady's husband just passed away— he had been ill for a long time. She cared for him herself and worked at cleaning jobs or whatever she could do to keep them going. The place where they were living is up for sale and Brownie just told me on the way over here that he heard its been sold. I don't know where she will go."

"Hmm, "mused Jenny, "I'll think about it. I don't know how I could possibly afford to pay anyone just now."

"Oh, my dear, no, I think she would just be happy for a place to stay and something to eat," explained Niki. "I was kind of thinking of those unused rooms upstairs."

"It might work," said Jenny. "What is she like?"

"Quiet, hard working, neat—probably in her fifties—I'm sure she would be a lot of help to you," answered Niki.

"Well, let me meet her Sunday," responded Jenny.

"Brownie after filling himself with cookies had left the table and gone into the back yard where the children were playing. He soon returned with Robbie helping him carry a sign. It was brightly painted with the words, "Jenny's Bakery" in large bold letters.

While he and Robbie went out front to put up the sign, Niki unwrapped a surprise gift for Jenny—material for curtains for the front windows of the bakery and enough of a matching material for tablecloths for the two little tables. The rest of the afternoon they cut and stitched, chatting and watching Jacqueline and Elizabeth as they played in and out of the house.

Jenny was pleased with the gift of material and thanked Niki most appreciatively, but firmly telling her in no uncertain terms that she would repay her for her kindness.

Sunday came so fast that Jenny could hardly believe it was here. She was a little nervous. After all, she had not been to a church service since her marriage to Jacque. He would not allow them to attend services without him and since he was rarely home on weekends, they never went to church. Jenny in the beginning used to ask Jacque about going, but it'd only caused trouble and usually ended with a slap across her face. This Sunday morning Jenny rose early, happy and excited and a little apprehensive. She was glad Niki and Brownie were coming for them. She didn't really want to go to a new church alone, the first time.

Jenny didn't want to think about serious things today. She had worked hard and everything was ready to begin her work early tomorrow, but today was a day of rest.

It looked like it was to be a warm sunny day. Jenny chose her white dress with the tiny lavender flowers. She fed and helped the children dress, brushing Elizabeth's long auburn hair around her fingers into ringlets. She smoothed Robbie's hair and checked his ears. Then she brushed Jacqueline's blonde curls and put on their new bonnets. Jenny's red hair was pulled up on her head into a bun, soft wisps making their way across her forehead and down the back of her neck.

Just as she put on her own bonnet and tied the bow under her chin, she heard the Brown's coming up the sidewalk. They looked different in their Sunday attire. Brownie had on a suit and tie and Niki was really attractive in a pale gray dress with a flowered bonnet neatly covering her graying hair.

Exchanges were made as to how grand everyone looked, then Niki produced a large picnic basket filled with delicious items for an after church dinner in the park. She would leave it in the coolness of Jenny's pantry and pick it up after services. She was apologetic about the food not being any match for Jenny's gourmet cooking but she was sure it was eatable anyway and Brownie agreed he had survived on it quite well all these years.

They walked the little distance from the bakery to the church. It was a warm, lovely, and spacious sanctuary. As they walked down the aisle with their friends to the pew—some heads turned and looked in their direction, but they were friendly stares and Jenny felt more at ease than she had thought she would.

Jenny enjoyed singing hymns with the congregation. The sermon delivered by the minister was soul searching, but lengthy. She tried to keep her thoughts on the message but couldn't help surveying with wonder the ornate fixtures and stained glass windows from the corner of her eyes. The elegant high ceilings and the resplendent beauty of the church's interior was quite breath taking. The crowd was large and Brownie's pew was about half way from the front. She tried not to be obvious in her glances about, but was suddenly surprised when she noticed in the row ahead on the other side, the young attorney Benjamin Forbes seated with a very charming young woman at his side. He glanced her way just then and smiled. Niki caught the smile and the one returned by Jenny.

"Do you know him?" whispered Niki to Jenny.

"Yes, we met very briefly," whispered Jenny in return.

"He's a fine young man," nodded Niki, "came from a rather affluent family. I think he just became a member of the bar."

"Shh," admonished Brownie with a kindly grin.

At the close of the services, Jenny was introduced to many people. It seemed the Brown's knew most everyone and wanted Jenny to meet them all. The minister and his wife welcomed Jenny and the children and stated they would be calling on them in a few days. Benjamin made himself known, welcoming them and introducing the lovely lady as his sister, Martha.

Benjamin couldn't seem to take his eyes off Jenny but just as he took courage to speak to her again, Niki interrupted by explaining to Jenny that she wanted her to meet Mrs. Ashton, the lady they had spoken to her about on Friday.

Jenny was immediately touched by the tired appearing woman looking so alone—sort of displaced. Not knowing how to approach the subject of employment, it was suggested that Niki bring Mrs. Ashton around to the bakery midweek and they could then talk about some kind of arrangement.

After picking up the picnic basket and catching a horse–drawn carriage, they set off for the park. Before long, they had spread a blanket in the shade and were soon partaking of Niki's generous picnic lunch. There were sandwiches, baked beans, fried chicken, crisp sweet pickles, and plenty of lemonade. Toward the end of the meal, Niki brought a melon from the basket and cut it into juicy slices for everyone to enjoy. It wasn't too great for Sunday clothes, but no matter, they would wash.

With lunch over and the few dishes packed away, it was sort of a lounging time. After a while when every one seemed rested from overeating, Brownie stated that he had a surprise for the children.

They picked up the blanket and sauntered slowly off through the enchanting park. People were everywhere. It was just a perfect day—neither too hot nor too cool.

Soon they approached a picturesque lagoon. Here was Brownie's surprise—the colorful swan boats. They were striking little boats made to depict swans. Each boat held four adults or children and were pedal–powered for a fifteen minute ride around the figure–eight shaped pond.

"Oh, how pretty," squealed Elizabeth with delight.

"Can we ride Mama, can we ride?" excitedly coaxed Robbie and Elizabeth, both jumping about with expectation.

"Oh course they can, right?" questioned Brownie of Jenny.

"I, well, what, I don't know," stammered Jenny clutching here throat.

"Don't worry," said Niki with an assuring pat, "they will be just fine. Brownie won't let anything happen to them. He'll take good care of them. Besides, the water is shallow. Come on we'll sit over here on the bench with Jacqueline and wait for them to return, all right?" questioned Niki with a growing concern for the strange expression on Jenny's face.

"All right," replied Jenny, her throat so dry she could barely speak and her head felt like it was spinning in circles.

Jenny stared as Brownie lifted Elizabeth into one of the boats. Robbie had already climbed aboard. As he lifted the little girl into the air, a gentle breeze caught her dress—white, billowy, flowing like soft white clouds. The boat rocked gently back and forth and her upturned face shone with a smile of expectancy. Suddenly, Jenny felt the scream coming from her lips, she tried to hold it back, but it wouldn't stop coming. What could she do?

"Mama, Mama, Mama," pierced the air, but oh it wasn't her—Oh thank goodness no—no, it was Jacqueline—Jacqueline was screaming, "Mama, Mama, Mama, me go too, me go too," she cried as the little boat had begun to pull away.

"Here," said Brownie reaching out for the toddler, "give her to me. She will be fine here on my lap."

"Is it okay?" asked Niki, looking at Jenny a little worried.

"I, I guess it will be all right," she answered dully—almost inaudibly.

As the little vessel begin to move and surge through the water, Jenny's mind was overcome with a childhood memory. She was eight or so—it was a hot Sunday afternoon. Paulette had been in a terrible mood all morning. In the afternoon, the two ladies who worked with Paulette had decided to cool off with a walk in the park. Thinking it might help Paulette's mood some, they had been granted permission for Jenny to accompany them. Jenny remembered how pleasant it had been to walk along the quiet paths. St. Louis had such pretty parks and she wasn't allowed this freedom very often. After a while they had wandered over to a pond when suddenly, two white swans came floating gracefully toward them. Oh, how beautiful Jenny had thought as she stood watching them glide toward her. Suddenly, as they approached her she had been gripped with such terror and loneliness that she began to shake and then sobs came and she couldn't stop. She wanted to scream, but the scream wouldn't come—only shaking and sobbing and finally after trying to console her and finding it was all to no avail, the poor frustrated ladies had taken her home. The best explanation they could give to Paulette was that Jenny was frightened by the swans. Paulette just sneered a half smile and stated that the child was afraid of everything.

It was after that experience, Jenny thought, when the nightmares had begun. She never could remember them to well. That is not until lately—lately—they seemed to stay with her more. It seemed they always started with soft white— something billowy, maybe clouds—she didn't know. She would be happy but then in a moment it would all change and terror would begin and she would try to scream, but the sound would not come forth. Sometimes in the last few weeks she would scream out loud and here head would ache, oh, it hurt so, like a sharp blow and she felt like she would smother to death.

The splash of the water caught her attention –they were back. Jenny had been in such deep thought that all conscious- ness of time had left her. The little boat made its way to the dock and Brownie handed Jacqueline to Niki.

"Oh, Mama! We had such a wonderful time," exclaimed Elizabeth excitedly as she and Robbie climbed ashore.

"Yes," laughed Brownie, "I think I have found me some sailing mates. They took to the water like old salts."

"Can we go again," asked Robbie hopefully.

"I don't think your Mama feels too well," interrupted Niki. "It's been a long day—perhaps we had better catch a carriage and start for home."

"What's wrong, Jenny?" asked Brownie, "You do look awfully pale."

"I'm sorry," Jenny answered, "I feel much better now, but I am a little tired."

"Well, I guess so," reasoned Brownie, "all the work you've been doing to get ready for tomorrow. It's enough to wear anyone out.

"Come on sailors," he teased calling to the children, "let's race to find a carriage." He picked up Jacqueline in his big arms and they hustled off together.

"Are you really feeling better?" inquired Niki as she and Jenny followed slowly behind.

"I really do—I am fine now," answered Jenny.

"Well you sure scared me," confided Niki, "you never said a word the whole time they were gone. You just stared after them like you'd seen a ghost or something. Thank goodness the color is finally coming back into your face."

By the time they arrived home Jenny was laughing and talking as much as anyone else. Niki insisted, however, that Jenny sit down in the parlor and let her and Elizabeth prepare for them a late snack. So, Jenny sat in the parlor with a cup of tea while Brownie tried to help Robbie and Jacqueline play a sailors tune on the piano keys.

It was good to be home—yes, she was glad she had come. Tonight she would rest. Tomorrow, its back to work...Jenny had much to do.

Chapter Ten

Monday morning at the new bakery had been a total success. Jenny awoke very early and with the preparation she had already made in advance, she had everything baked and the kitchen in good shape by the time she turned the front door sign to show "open".

However, Jenny had not contemplated the great number of patrons desirous of her bread and pastry items that she so deliciously and intriguingly displayed in her show cases. Everything was sold out before noon and although extremely pleased with the first days' profits, she knew that if the amount of her clientele would continue or increase she would certainly need some help and fast.

The Brown's were surprised to see a closed sign on the front door when they stopped by a little after noon.

"What happened, Jenny?" asked Niki, "didn't you open this morning?" She had in her hand fresh flowers for the tables cut from her garden.

"It was just a tremendous surge of people," explained Jenny excitedly. "I pulled up the shades and opened the door and there must have been about twenty people on their way to work and as soon as I waited on them I looked and the two little tables were filled. I didn't think about having menus so it took time to tell them each what was available to order. I poured coffee and tea, waited on the counter and the people just kept coming until everything was sold out. All the loaves of bread were gone in an hour."

"There must not be another bakery around for miles," laughed Jenny happily as she finished combing Jacqueline's hair. "Robbie helped with breakfast for him and the girls, it was all prepared but we're a little behind on dressing."

She fastened Jacqueline's shoes and as the children went out to play, Brownie, Niki, and Jenny sat down over a pot of coffee in the big kitchen mulling over the possibilities of a seemingly opportune situation.

After much talk and planning it was decided that Niki would come over early enough in the mornings to run the store part of the bakery until Jenny could find someone else, leaving Jenny free to work in the kitchen full time.

If Mrs. Ashten would be interested in moving into the upstairs rooms, she could assist with baking chores and also help with the children. Brownie was sure he could clean and make any repairs that needed to be done upstairs before he went back to his fishing boat.

On Wednesday afternoon, Florence Ashten came by the bakery as Jenny had requested. Niki brought her back to the kitchen and hastily returned to the front where Brownie had now set up two more tables for customers. Jenny wiped the dough from her hands and gestured for the lady to be seated.

"As you can see," smiled Jenny, "we are very busy—of course, we don't know if this rush will continue, but it has been like this since we opened."

"Yes, it was busy when I came through out there," said Mrs. Ashten. "Niki had her hands full."

"I don't know what Niki told you," continued Jenny. "I have three small children, although the two oldest are a great help to me. Elizabeth and Robbie both seem older then their six and seven years of age. Elizabeth is trying to help Niki right now and Robbie is upstairs giving Brownie a hand. However, I do have a three–year old and if this volume of business continues I will need help."

"Have you ever worked in a bakery?" asked Jenny.

"No," replied Mrs. Ashten, "but, I like to bake and I learn quickly. I work hard at whatever I do—I am in good health and I can start work as soon as you would like. I really need the job and I am willing to work for room and board. The place where my husband and I lived for ten years was sold last week and I really don't know where to go. Everything is so expensive."

"Do you have any furniture?" questioned Jenny.

"Yes, a little," answered Mrs. Ashten. "I was thinking of maybe selling it."

"Well, I'll tell you," said Jenny, "If you work for me it will probably be a diversified job—part time sitter, some cleaning, up early helping me bake, maybe helping Niki out front—six days a week with Sunday's off. The small apartment upstairs would be yours free—all the food you want and wages commensurate with the profits of the bakery. If you decide to take the job, your furniture would be welcomed, as the apartment has few furnishings in it. We can go upstairs now and look it over if you would like."

"That won't be necessary," responded Mrs. Ashten, "I will be happy to accept. When could I start?" she asked with tears of relief in her eyes.

"How about tomorrow," said Jenny, "I think everything is about ready upstairs and if you can get someone to move your things to the apartment you can take possession immediately."

The tired look of uncertainty seemed to subside some from Mrs. Ashten's face.

"That sounds good to me," she smiled and with a sigh of relief continued, "I didn't want to say anything, but I was told yesterday that I had until the end of the week and then my things would be set out on the street. It isn't much but it's all I have. This is really an answer to prayer. God does answer doesn't He? I just feel that such a tremendous burden has been taken from me. I hardly know what to say."

"Yes, God does answer prayer," agreed Jenny, "and I think you're going to like it here..." but before Jenny could finish her sentence, Jacqueline came running into the kitchen. She had been upstairs with Robbie and Brownie.

"Mama, Mama," cried out the little girl, "Uncle Brownie wants to know—can 'ou come up," she pointed toward the upstairs.

"All right," answered Jenny, "Come with me Mrs. Ashten."

"Please call me Flo," offered Mrs. Ashten, "I feel more comfortable with that."

"Okay, Flo it is," agreed Jenny as they made their way to the upstairs.

Jenny was amazed at the way the little apartment had changed since Monday when she had first seen it. Brownie had fixed windows, painted walls, removed boxes, and accumulated junk and it looked very nice.

Flo beamed with satisfaction as she looked around. There was at the entrance a little sitting room with windows overlooking the street, a tiny kitchen, a small bedroom and Brownie was busy installing a water closet like the one downstairs in the washroom.

"You know," declared Brownie, "we are so close to finishing that I probably could get a few men from the church and move you in tonight, if you like, Flo. What do you think?"

It was agreed upon and Flo moved into the cozy little apartment that evening.

The children and Flo were ideal companions. She proved to be not only capable, but kind and understanding with the children and a close friend to Jenny. She proved herself to be very efficient in whatever she was asked to do and Jenny was glad that she had come to live with them.

When school started in the fall, Jenny entered both Robbie and Elizabeth. They were able to attend the same school to begin with and seemed to adjust very well not having attended before. Robbie turned eight in August and Elizabeth seven in September just after school began.

The bakery seemed to be a complete success and Niki who at first thought her work would be temporary had continued to come every day. She seemed to really be enjoying it and Jenny had discovered that Niki was a good manager and bookkeeper.

Jenny also hired a girl by the name of Mary to come in the afternoon and help. The rent was paid in advance and from the first week, she had been able to pay Flo and Niki a small salary. Jenny and Flo were up early every morning but Sunday, working side by side in the kitchen until the children awoke and then one or the other would get Robbie and Elizabeth off to school.

Jacqueline played happily about the house or in the small back yard with everyone there to watch over her. She was very contented with her situation. Robbie and Elizabeth returned each day telling Jacqueline all that had happened and how exciting it was to be in school and their accounts of the day's events holding her spellbound.

Supper was a happy time. The bakery closed at five and Jenny and Flo would have the meal on the table just as the closed sign was displayed. Often Niki would stay and eat with them if Brownie was out on the fishing boat and if the boats were in dock he might show up to join them.

The days flew past rapidly and before they knew it, Thanksgiving was almost upon them. If Jenny thought business was brisk in August now it really picked up. Brownie had installed more efficient ovens for them, and they were now turning out pies and cakes, along with breads and cookies, and many other delicious baked goods.

Benjamin managed to drop by the bakery often. He would stop and chat with Niki and have a cup of coffee at one of the little tables. Somehow, he would always end up in the warm and inviting kitchen just to say hello to Flo and Jenny.

On one of these occasions, his sister, Martha, accompanied him, and from that time on a friendship grew between Jenny and Benjamin's sister. Martha admired the younger woman. Most of her friends were spoiled and selfish. Even her married friends thought only of parties and travel and expensive clothes, not that there was anything wrong with those things but these seemed to be their priorities in life.

Jenny was so different—she never went to parties, thought little about traveling, and not overly concerned about fashions. Her life was her children and the success of the small bakery. She cared about Flo and was concerned for her welfare.

Martha had always had what ever she needed or wanted supplied for her and she could proudly take her place with the best of Boston's social finest.

Jenny had nothing but sheer determination to succeed with her natural talents and the abilities she had acquired.

Martha was also very certain that Benjamin felt more for Jenny than admiration. She was two years older than Benjamin and very protective of her younger brother. She did not want him to be hurt in any way, but she could see no reciprocation of his affection for Jenny. In fact, she did not even believe that Jenny was aware of anything between her and Benjamin but friendship and considered his attention as only that of a friend.

One early afternoon, Martha dropped by the bakery.

"Good day, Flo," she greeted as she stepped into the spicy mouth watering aroma of the kitchen.

Flo looked up from a sheet of hot molasses cookies she was just taking out of the oven.

"Hi, Miss Forbes—how are you today?" asked Flo as she quickly removed the cookies from the sheet onto the cupboard.

"Just fine," she answered. "Is Jenny around here some-where?" she inquired.

"She just stepped back to check on Jacqueline who is taking a nap," responded Flo.

"Oh, those look so good," admired Martha with anticipation looking at the freshly baked cookies.

"Help yourself," offered Flo, as she held out a plate of sugary cookies for Martha.

"Oh, I can't," explained Martha with fortitude, "I am really hoping to steal Jenny away for the afternoon for some shopping, and then on to dinner at a splendid restaurant. I want to be wicked and splurge on the French pastry, so I had better pass on the cookies."

"Oh Jenny, there you are," said Martha as Jenny came through the doorway into the kitchen.

"Well, hello, Martha," greeted Jenny. "Have you been here long?"

"No," answered Martha, "but, I was just telling Flo my intention of talking you into changing your dress, putting on your coat and having dinner with me in an elegant restaurant. Of course, after we have spent the afternoon shopping.

"Oh, I don't think I can," responded Jenny hesitantly.

"Now look, you have Flo right here and Niki out front and I saw Brownie on his way in when I came, plus Mary will be here shortly," argued Martha persistently, "Now, they can certainly take over for one afternoon and care for the little ones. It will do you good to get away."

"Jenny, why don't you go," agreed Flo, "we will be just fine. The children won't be home until late in the afternoon and Jacqueline isn't any trouble. You go on and have a nice time. We already have supper started and no one is going hungry around this place."

"Well, I guess you all would be alright," smiled Jenny with some reservation as she continued, "It would be nice."

"Grab a cookie and some tea while I change, Martha, I'll just be a minute," shouted Jenny as she hurried off.

"Oh, okay, I might as well," acquiesced Martha with a resolute sigh while taking a cup from the cupboard.

"You can eat all the sweets you want Miss Martha—you're so nice and thin—you certainly don't have anything to worry about," chuckled Flo good naturedly.

Before Martha's cup of tea was finished, Jenny had returned and was ready to go.

Jenny had never seen such shops. Martha knew exactly where to go and apparently was well known by the shopkeepers who called her by name.

Martha purchased what ever pleased her and kept coaxing Jenny to just try on a few things. Jenny refused, but did acquire a warm shawl for Flo to be given as a Christmas gift and she looked at some gloves for Niki. It was in a children's shop that Jenny couldn't resist buying a few needed articles of clothing for the children. She also selected a few toys from several that she liked. Without her knowledge, Martha instructed the sales clerks to wrap everything Jenny liked and that would be her surprise come Christmas day.

Time slipped away and they shopped longer than they intended. It was nearly six o'clock when they arrived to dine. They checked their packages and were seated at a table cold and hungry after their long afternoon of shopping.

"I am really glad I came," affirmed a tired but happy Jenny as they warmed themselves with hot cups of tea. "Thank you for inviting me, Martha."

"I'm glad you were able to come," replied Martha, "Now, you order anything you like from the menu—my treat."

"Oh, I can't let you do that," objected Jenny.

"Now, just wait a minute, Jenny," retorted Martha, "Benjamin and I have had lunch at your house twice last week and dinner the night before last. This is just pay back time, so please don't give me an argument."

"Well, I guess if you put it like that," smiled Jenny in agreement.

Dinner was perfect with white tablecloths, long stemmed crystal glasses, and real china. Martha chose lobster, but Jenny had never tasted of it before and wasn't so sure about ordering it. She settled for a steak and it was most delectable.

Since they had arrived, the restaurant gradually had filled to capacity. They were almost finished with dessert when Jenny could not help notice that a good looking gentleman who had been seated at a table a short distance away was staring at her. She tried to ignore him, but each time she would look in his direction, he would turn his head and look away.

"What's wrong, Jenny?" questioned Martha sensing a sudden change in her friend's mood.

"Don't turn around, please, Martha," whispered Jenny, "but, there is a gentleman at the second table behind you who keeps staring at me. At first, I thought he might be looking at someone else, but now I am becoming a bit uncomfortable."

"Yes, I can see your cheeks are flushed," replied Martha as she turned to see who was annoying her friend.

"Martha! Don't turn around," cringed Jenny in embarrassment.

"Well, I don't care," responded Martha with indignation as she glanced sideways to get a better view without being obvious, "which table did you say?"

"Never mind, he's getting up. I think he is leaving," sighed Jenny in relief.

The well–dressed gentleman came toward them.

"Good evening, Miss Forbes," he said, nodding to Martha with a cool but amicable glance as he passed her chair.

Then he faced Jenny with an examining gaze, hesitating, almost as if to speak, but not finding words to say he moved on looking perplexed as he left.

"Do you know him, Martha?" asked Jenny looking bewildered.

"Well, I know who he is—his mother and my grandmother were friends, but I don't know him very well," answered Martha with some uncertainty.

"Jenny, I think he was quite taken with you," she smiled.

"Has he left yet?" questioned Jenny, turning her head cautiously in the direction he had taken.

"Yes, he has gone," answered Martha. "I am sorry he upset you. He certainly is highly respected and I am sure not intentionally ill mannered. I have heard said from someone not totally reliable, that he has been known to imbibe now and again, but I don't believe he was intoxicated.

"You know," explained Martha thoughtfully as the two young ladies moved away from their table, Alex Gordon is a very wealthy man. He and his mother, Rosetta, own a ship building company. There isn't a single woman in Boston who wouldn't be thrilled to receive that much attention from such an eligible bachelor."

"What did you say his name is?" inquired Jenny with increased interest.

"Alex Gordon, have you heard of him?" asked Martha.

"No, I guess not," said Jenny soberly, but, she remained very quiet on the trip home. Martha felt it was because it had been a long day for Jenny. She knew how early Jenny rose to begin her workday and with the shopping and all they had accomplished she was sure Jenny was very tired.

Martha left not thinking too much more about the incident at the restaurant. Jenny did, in fact she thought about it long into the night. Why had Alex Gordon stared at her so intently? She had traveled half-way across the country in search of Paulette's family roots—was it a coincidence that someone with the same name as that engraved on the locket became so intriguingly fascinated by her presence? Jenny looked nothing like Paulette. He had stared at her with such incredulity that she became startled. Martha thought Alex's fixed look was one of earnest admiration, but Jenny felt it was something else. It was a look of puzzlement, almost as if he knew her.

Jenny tossed about so much she woke Jacqueline who slept beside her in the big bed.

"I'm sorry sweetheart," soothed Jenny, "go back to sleep."

Niki and Brownie had brought a child's single bed for Elizabeth and although it was in the same room as Jenny's she would be more comfortable in her own bed.

"O, Lord, help me to sleep," she prayed as Jacqueline drifted off to sleep again.

"I think I am losing my sanity," groaned Jenny, "I seem so normal around people, but in my mind strange unidentifiable thoughts sometimes hold me spellbound leaving me with unexplained feelings.

Finally, she slept, but Alex Gordon's face drifted in and out of her haunting dreams of vague, unreal, and remote identities.

"Lixie—Lixie," she whispered softly in her sleep.

Chapter Eleven

The weather turned blustery and cold immediately after Thanksgiving. Snow fell almost every day and the brisk ocean wind blew harsh and biting.

Trying to contain the children's exuberance and excitement in anticipation of Christmas was impossible. It was made especially more difficult as packages wrapped in bright paper and bows grew higher, under and around the tree each day. Gifts continued to arrive almost daily as the Browns and Forbes could not repress their pleasure in purchasing things for the children.

Brownie with Robbie's help and careful consideration selected a fresh cut fir tree. With great enthusiasm, they had carried it into the parlor for a memorable evening of decorating.

Niki and Flo helped Elizabeth and Robbie string long strands of popcorn and bright, red cranberries that Brownie expertly wound through the green boughs of the tree. Martha and Jenny in light–hearted conversation worked in the kitchen, stirring hot sugar syrup over big bowls of popcorn as Ben rolled up his sleeves and with buttered hands pressed the puffed white kernels into delicious sweet balls of confection.

Martha brought several trinkets for the tree, one of them being an angel for the top–most branch. It was garbed in a white gown with a pale blue sash. Golden hair adorned its head and the wings appeared to be made of real feathers.

"O, Mama, is it a weel angle," questioned Jacqueline with wide–eyed amazement at its beauty.

"No, Honey," explained Jenny, "it is very lovely, but I am sure real angels are much larger than that."

"O, I wove her Mama, she is so pitty," said Jacqueline intently gazing at the angel with her eyes shinning in wonderment. Tottering on her tip toes, trying not to lose sight of it as Benjamin was placing it on the top of the tree.

"Here, Sweetheart," declared Ben as he removed the object of Jacqueline's admiration and placed it in the child's tiny hands.

A smile of wonder came over her little face as she gently touched the cloth gown adorning the 'tree top' angel.

"Soft," she said as she felt the golden hair. The child had seen so little of anything pretty. Christmas had not been a time to remember with Jacque. Jenny thought with a shudder how hard she had tried to make Christmas pleasant for the children last year. Jacque had come home drunk the day before Christmas. She and the children had cut a tree down and attempted to decorate it. Jacque smashed the tree and tossed it outside into the snow. He had ranted and raved like a maniac for the next two days continuing to fortify his wicked temper with another bottle whenever he started to wind down. Jenny had made a rag doll for each of the girls from some scraps of worn cloth. She also had managed to secretly arrange to do some of Mrs. Shultz's baking in preparation for the holiday season while Jacque was gone on one of his trips. When Mr. Schultz came to pick up the baked goods Jenny had asked him if he would purchase Robbie a book instead of payment in money. She explained it was to be a Christmas gift and that Robbie would really enjoy a book about sailing ships. Unable to find one he instead bought an illustrated Story of the Bible. Jenny knew Robbie would love it, but he never received it nor the girls their rag dolls, because when Jacque found out what she had done without his knowledge he threw them all into the fire. Then in a rage, he smashed Jenny's face with his fist and knocked her about the room. Jenny was sure she would die that day.

"'ook, Mama," called Jacqueline shaking Jenny to get her attention. "Benamin gave me the angle—to keep—she's mine," smiled the child up to Jenny with a smile not unlike an angel herself.

"Oh, how nice," remarked Jenny glancing at Benjamin. "How thoughtful and kind he was. So, we have a tree without an angel," she laughed.

"No, Mama," interrupted the child as she explained, "Me put pitty angle on the tweetop 'til twee is done then Jac–a–win keeps her."

"Say, that sounds good to me," declared Martha, seeing I am the one who bought the angel. She is yours all year Jacqueline, but each Christmas we will enjoy looking at her on the top of the tree."

Many years later as the closely knit family and friends sat in front of a crackling fireplace enjoying the beauty of another fine Christmas, they reflected with fond memories upon the little angel that still, after many Holiday Seasons adorned the top of a splendid tree across the room.

Just as Benjamin accepted Jacqueline's offering of her angel from her outstretched hands and placed it on top of the tree, Flo brought in a tray of hot cups of cocoa and everyone sat down to rest from tree trimming to enjoy the delicious hot drink.

The busy days before Christmas passed quickly for the adults, but not quickly enough for the children. It seemed to them that Christmas would never come. They tried to count the packages to see how many there were without touching or disturbing them.

"Mama, you have to keep Jacqueline away from the tree," explained Elizabeth with a worried look. "When she thinks we are not looking she shakes the packages to try and tell what's in them. She is messing them up something terrible while Robbie and I are in school."

"They look all right to me," replied Jenny, then looking at Jacqueline, "Jacqueline, are you shaking the presents under the tree?" questioned Jenny as the little girl toddled by. Christmas is almost here so please don't shake the packages anymore."

"I von't," exclaimed Jacqueline as she scooted off toward the kitchen with Jenny in hot pursuit both laughing and pretending Jacqueline was in deep trouble.

Jenny caught the child in a big embrace and swung her around in a fast twirl.

"Do it again Mama, do it again," squealed Jacqueline in delight.

"You be a good little girl and leave the tree and packages alone," scolded Jenny in good nature but with a stern voice that Jacqueline respected.

"Flo—how are we coming with the pies?" asked Jenny turning her attention to business.

"They're comin' just fine. We should be through baking pies late tomorrow.

"Good," said Jenny, "and if all goes well, the day before Christmas we will only have bread to bake. Everything else should be done."

"You have been a tremendous help Flo, you and Niki, I couldn't have done it all without your generous help.

Flo looked pleased as she poured mincemeat into several pie shells and put them in the oven to bake.

"Thank you, Jenny, " she said as she wiped a tear from her cheek. It sure has become a home for me and you and the children my family."

"We've all been through a lot," replied Jenny with empathy, "but I think it is going to be a really nice Christmas It will be a pleasure to have Christmas dinner at the Forbes' house and it was so good of them to invite all of us including Niki and Brownie.

"Yes, I am looking forward to it," agreed Flo. "They sure are nice Christian folks."

The Browns stayed over Christmas Eve not wanting to miss out on the opening of gifts Christmas morning.

Jenny put down thick quilts on the parlor rug for the children. They thought it was so wonderful to sleep by the tree all night. Jenny slept in Robbie's bed and gave hers to the Browns.

They sang Christmas Carols and Niki made taffy for a taffy pull.

Finally, Brownie took the big Bible from the parlor table where Jenny left it open all the time. Jenny had found it among all the many books on the shelves in Robbies' room.

Jenny and Niki, Flo, Robbie, Elizabeth and Jacqueline gathered around Brownie as he read the story of Jesus birth in Bethlehem from the second chapter of Luke.

It snowed hard Christmas Eve and Benjamin arrived before noon Christmas day with horses and sleigh for the ride to dinner.

"Benjamin, come and see—come and see," called Elizabeth from the side door leading to the kitchen.

The children did not know where or who had brought them all the wonderful gifts, but their excitement and joy could not be contained today. Even Robbie who was usually more reserved helped escort Benjamin into the parlor leaving the driver waiting in the sleigh.

The parlor seemed overflowing with various shaped and brightly wrapped gifts. A sleigh for Robbie, one each for Elizabeth and Jacqueline and the most beautiful dolls ever seen, a set of play dishes in a tiny cupboard, a little table with four chairs made by Brownie, doll clothes for the two dolls that Martha had cut and sewn from material she had and quilts and pillows for doll cradles she had purchased especially made for them.

Brownie had fashioned a replica of a three–masted sailing vessel for which Niki helped make the sails as a special gift for Robbie and Benjamin could not resist purchasing a wind–up train for Robbie, which actually ran around an oval track.

Niki got carried away in her eager endeavor of making clothes for the children. She provided them with everything they would need in the line of clothing until they outgrew what she had made and purchased for them. Of course, the way they were growing that might not be too far in the future. At least Jacqueline could wear Elizabeth's outgrown things.

Jenny was in a state of delightful bewilderment as she couldn't believe all the wonderful things the Browns and Forbes had given to them. The few little things she had given in return seemed so paltry, but she knew they had given from their hearts and it was the most extraordinary and memorable Christmas anyone could ever have.

Flo and Jenny were not forgotten either by their benevolent friends. Although they received many wonderful gifts, it was the love and warm heartfelt friendship of their gracious friends that they cherished most.

It was a rather disorderly group that set out for the Forbes, but it was a happy one as they crowded into the two–seated sleigh and snuggled down as they were covered with warm, heavy blankets.

"Don't cuber my baby," said Jacqueline as she lovingly cradled her new doll all wrapped carefully in its blanket.

Jenny had not been to the Forbes' home before. She really didn't know what to expect. She was sure they were affluent but in many ways, they seemed so common.

The house was large and old. Not as grand appearing as Jenny might have thought. However, upon entering, it was lovely and its grandeur was evident.

There were two adjoining parlors one with an adjacent library, each with long fireplaces with blazing logs that gave off a scintillating illumination and warmth to the rooms. The mantles were draped with holiday greenery and the high stairway in the open front hall was wrapped with holly and boughs of pine.

The largest Christmas tree Jenny had ever seen greeted her with captivating awe as she entered one of the parlors and looked in wonder as it was adorned from floor to ceiling with beautiful ornaments and tapers.

The huge dinning room table was set with beautiful china placed on a delicate Irish linen cloth. A set of logs burned brightly in a small fireplace giving a soft warm glow to the room.

As the merry company sat down to the splendid meal, grace was said by Benjamin who sat at the head of the long dinning room table. Somehow, Jenny thought he looked rather uncomfortable in the role as head of the family, but he accepted his duty and did it well.

Martha was seated with the guests along the sides having relinquished her place at the other end of the table in honor of a great aunt who was visiting them for the holidays.

Two maids served dinner. They were dressed in black frocks with crisp white aprons and dainty caps. A butler helped and cleared away each course. It was a sumptuous meal. Jenny was sure she had never seen so much food before and such gracious cordiality even when Jacqueline upset her milk and the glass rolled onto the floor.

Jenny had known before that day that Martha and Benjamin had been brought up by their grandparents, now deceased, their own parents having both died young. What she didn't really know is how truly caring they were about the needs of others. She learned that both were very busily involved in legitimate good causes to benefit the poor and needy. Martha was president of the church's Missionary Society—heading up an extensive work that helped support many missions, foreign and at home. She also worked with a group that cared for those in need in the Boston area, especially at Christmas.

Benjamin helped in a local mission, distributing food and necessities and sharing Christ with the men as they came in for sustenance. He also volunteered his services at an orphanage for boys one night a week.

So, it was that Christmas afternoon, after the family dinner was over that the large old house was turned over to entertain and give some Christmas cheer to several boys from the orphanage and a misfortunate widow and her seven children who had been left without the means for Christmas.

The dinning table was cleared, and the buffet was set with trays of ham, smoked fish, and sliced turkey, warm breads and dainty relishes and jelly, and hot cider and cocoa with steamed pudding with sauces.

There were gifts for each and all, toys for the children along with warm coats and galoshes, scarves and gloves.

"The wonderful part of it all," Martha explained to Jenny, "we care for them throughout the year, not just at Christmas."

Soon, the happy sound of merry voices filled the crisp night air and the full moon brightly shone on each happy group as Benjamin and his driver returned several times and piled the sleigh high with gifts and people taking them safely to their respective homes.

Last, but certainly not least, it was Jenny's and the three sleepy children's turn for a ride home. Benjamin had taken the Browns home with one of the groups of boys, as the orphanage was near the wharves where the Browns resided.

"Look how the snow sparkles and shines like crystal," observed Elizabeth with delight as the sleigh bells jingled merrily as they progressed along the snow covered streets.

There were many cutters and sleighs filled with happy people gliding by in the night with shouts of Merry Christmas ringing through the night air as they passed with lanterns glowing.

Even Jacqueline was determined to keep her eyes open— not wanting to miss a thing on this joyous Christmas night, but long before they reached the little bakery, she had fallen asleep in her mother's arms.

The delightful ride in the sleigh with Jenny at his side passed too swiftly for Benjamin, but all good things must come and go and the night was preparing for a new day.

Benjamin helped Flo and Jenny, carrying the children into the house and then quietly bid them all good night. For him it had been an almost perfect day.

Chapter Twelve

Brownie's prediction that Jenny's cookies would be a winner came true. In fact not only her cookies, but it seemed anything Jenny baked and everything she offered for sale to her increasing clientele sold rapidly—from pies to cakes, doughnuts, or bread—whatever she put on the counters were purchased by her customers.

The beginning of the New Year 1904 was off to a splendid start for the little bakery, having not been in existence even a year and yet they were seeing a good profit.

With his fishing trawlers in dry dock for the winter, Brownie had been a great help around the bakery. He busied himself with repairs and improvements about the place and even waited on customers some. He and Robbie might slip out, after Robbie returned from school, for a bit of ice skating but always arrived home in time for the evening meal.

It had been difficult at first for Robbie and Elizabeth to catch up in their studies at school. Jenny had been their only teacher until they arrived in Boston. The first term had required such effort on everyone's part but they seemed to be showing improvement.

"Mama," said Robbie one morning at breakfast. "Do you remember saying that if the bakery was a success, that I might be able to study on the violin? I still would like that if we could afford a teacher," he explained with a wistful tone in his voice.

Jenny glanced at the serious expression on the face of her young son sitting across the table from her, but her attention was on Elizabeth who was intently pouring syrup over her pancakes.

"I remember you said that Mama," declared Elizabeth as she attempted to see how much syrup her pancakes would hold without running off the plate. "He talks to the violin, don't you Robbie," she added as she filed her mouth with a choice serving of pancake and syrup. "Hmm, that's good," she stated licking her lips.

"Elizabeth, your spilling the syrup, be careful," admonished Jenny, "and yes I do remember telling you that we might be able to let you take some lessons, Robbie. Do you really think you would be interested?" she questioned.

"Elizabeth! You're making a mess," scolded Jenny.

"I am making a gingerbread pancake," explained Elizabeth with a giggle.

"Me 'ant un too," clamored Jacqueline, "make me un too Lizebit—div me cherup Lizebit."

"No, Jacqueline," demanded Jenny. "You girls are getting sticky syrup all over."

"Mama," interrupted Robbie determined to be heard.

"What, Robbie?" questioned Jenny just as Jacqueline picked up the pitcher of sticky syrup and accidentally upset its contents over herself and the table.

Elizabeth broke into laughter running from the table to return with a cloth and made an attempt to wipe up the sticky mess. It was a mess, requiring a complete change of clothes for Jacqueline.

By the time Jenny returned to the kitchen, Flo had wiped the table clean and Elizabeth and Robbie were ready to go out the door to school. But, Robbie was not to be put off easily.

"Mama, can I or not?" asked the boy as he stood waiting for Flo to hand him his lunch pail.

"Can you or not what?" retorted Jenny crossly.

"I, I want to learn how to play the violin," he said with a determined set of his jaw.

"But you have so much school work to do in order to catch up with your class and practicing on the violin would take a great deal of time," explained Jenny calming herself a little.

"I would like to try," replied the boy with a glitter of hope in his eyes.

"He talks to it all the time and tells it he will make music come out of those strings," smiled Elizabeth, giving her brother a hug, from which he gently pulled away.

"Elizabeth, sometimes you have a big mouth," spouted Robbie.

"Robbie, don't be rude to your sister," reprimanded Jenny. "Why don't we wait until the end of the term at school," continued Jenny, "and if you catch up and do well, then we will consider it, but you must keep your school work up at all times regardless."

"All right," said Robbie in disappointment but with inner determination that he would bring his work up to date fueled by a longing to draw that bow across those strings and hear it make beautiful music.

Flo handed the children their lunch pails and they hurried off to school.

"Oh, Jenny, I almost forgot," said Flo, as she was beginning to clear the breakfast table, "Martha stopped by to see you last night, but you had gone to school to pick up the children. She left you an envelope—something about an invitation to a party."

"She did?" asked Jenny, "Where is it?"

"I laid it there on the desk in the parlor. I meant to tell you first thing, but it slipped my mind," explained Flo apologetically as she went to get the envelope. "Here it is."

It was already open and Jenny pulled the beautifully engraved paper from the envelope. The invitation was addressed to Martha and Benjamin Forbes. They were invited to attend a Valentine's Ball in the Grand Ballroom at the Gordon Mansion. They could each bring a guest of their choosing. It was signed by Rosetta and Alexander Gordon.

Martha had added a note inviting Jenny as her special guest and explaining it was the social event of the year. However, it was RSVP so please to let her know as soon as possible and hoping very much that she would be interested and accept.

"A party at the Gordon Mansion," said Jenny aloud in dismay.

"It's an invitation to a party?" inquired Flo observing Jenny's sudden change of expression.

"Yes! A big party at some very influential people's home," answered Jenny excitedly as she begin to fell the magnitude of what this invitation meant.

"Sounds nice. Who are they?" Flo questioned with reserve, not fully understanding the importance of the moment for Jenny.

"Why, Alex and Rosetta Gordon are very wealthy people. They own a ship building company on the waterfront her in Boston. Martha said they were the elite of the social community of the city."

"Oh, yes, I have heard of them. They have a huge estate on the outskirts of town," acknowledged Flo with recollection, then adding, "Well, Benjamin and Martha are kind of wealthy themselves. They just don't act like it toward others I guess. It's real nice of them to ask you to go along with them. Not many people like us would ever get the chance to go to some place like that."

Jenny had put the Gordons out of her mind for awhile, but as Flo continued speaking about them, a chill passed over Jenny and she clasped her arms about herself in a shiver.

"Are you cold?" Flo asked, noticing Jenny's bearing. "I think it is warm in here with the oven's going and all. I am almost too warm myself."

"No, yes—no," stammered Jenny thoughtfully, "I am not cold, I just had a sudden chill for some reason."

The subject of the ball was dropped until that afternoon when Martha came scurrying in asking with elated anticipation, "Jenny did you get my note?"

"Yes, I did," replied Jenny. "But, I don't know—I really don't know if I would be comfortable at such a function. I wouldn't even know how to conduct myself."

"Oh, yes—you will be fine—well maybe not—I don't know, I don't really think I really know how to conduct myself at such an elaborate function, but it's something you don't want to miss. It is without a doubt the most elegant social affair you will ever see in all of your life. I am not going to allow you to miss it. Besides, " she teasingly cajoled, "don't you want to see Alex Gordon again?"

"Not really," replied Jenny unconvincingly, "besides I have absolutely nothing to wear. I mean nothing."

"My dear," soothed Martha, "do you really think I would let you go without attire suitable for the occasion? The ball is some time away and we will have my dress maker come tomorrow and start fitting you."

"I couldn't possible afford it myself, nor could I allow you to have it done for me," stated Jenny with dismay.

"Well, then," concluded Martha, not to be put off so easily, you shall have one of my own gowns and we will have it altered to fit you."

Jenny was a good two inches shorter than Martha and smaller in frame.

"I couldn't allow you to do that either," argued Jenny.

"Oh, please say you will," pleaded Martha. "It would be a big favor to me as I really want to go, but not alone. Benjamin cannot attend as he has an important convention in New York City the week of the ball."

The look on Martha's face convinced Jenny that she was genuinely sincere and desirous for her to go. Jenny wanted to go—perhaps she would find some answers to her questions concerning herself—yes, she needed to go, and that settled it.

So, it was the next afternoon that Jenny was measured and fitted to one of the most luxurious of Martha's gowns. Jenny was hoping for a white, her favorite, but it wasn't in Martha's wardrobe. Martha selected a stunning green from the many frocks piled high on her bed. It would be perfect—embellishing her ivory skin, the soft green of her eyes, and the deep amber of her hair.

In the events of the following days, Jenny was not able to think anymore of the Gordons, or Martha's green gown. All that became unimportant in the light of what happened shortly thereafter.

The pond behind Dexter School where Robbie and Elizabeth both attended was frozen. All the children used it for skating and sledding during recess and lunch hour.

Benjamin and Martha had given Robbie a sleigh for Christmas, which he had taken to school almost every day. He and Elizabeth took turns pulling each other along the snowy paths. Jenny certainly had no idea of any impending danger it presented.

Some of the boys decided to climb up the hill behind the school on lunch hour and then slide all the way down the hill onto the pond below. Robbie went along with his new sled.

It was kind of rough walking up the incline of the steep hill, but once on the top it seemed like a good slide all the way down the hill onto the smooth surface of the frozen pond below. A couple of the boys went first, plunging down the hillside together at a super speed, then flying out over the icy pond and ending abruptly in a burst of laughter in a snow bank at the edge of the pond.

"Come on Robbie. Your next," they yelled as they jumped up and dusted the snow off their clothing.

Down the hill Robbie flew like a flash of light in the bright sunlight. The bumpy ruts near the bottom of the hill set him flying headlong into the air, landing with a loud crack in a spot on the pond, which had become softened by the warm sun. The force of Robbie's sled plunged him through the thin ice into the frigid murky waters.

If it had not been for the swift work of the school's groundskeeper, Robbie probably would have drowned. He saw the boy come speeding down the steep hill, and heard the distressed calls from the other boys. Somehow, with quick responsive reflex action, he managed to pull the lad to safety. He carried Robbie into the school where he was stripped of his wet clothing and wrapped in warm blankets by the fire. He was bruised and shaken, but aside from being very cold, seemed all right.

It wasn't until early the next morning that Jenny was awakened by Robbie's loud breathing. Rising quickly, she did what she could for him, applying the methods with which she was familiar, and at first light summoned the doctor.

The physician explained that Robbie had developed a rather severe chest cold and left him some foul tasting medicine that Robbie was sure would cure anything.

However, throughout the day, Robbie seemed to grow worse, and by early evening, he was burning up with fever and had great difficulty breathing.

Benjamin had come by the bakery in the afternoon and left hurriedly, returning sometime later with a specialist in medicine from Harvard.

The specialist took no time in determining that Robbie had double pneumonia. He was doubtful of the boy's recovery, and summoned for another colleague to be brought to the house.

Robbie slipped into semi–consciousness. The Browns and Flo tried to comfort Jenny but she would not be comforted.

"He can't die—he just can't," she cried as Benjamin tried to talk to her with comforting but encouraging words.

Martha was doing all she could to console Elizabeth and Jacqueline as they whimpered and cried not fully understanding the situation.

"I just won't accept this," blurted Jenny over and over again.

She told Flo to close the bakery and keep it closed until Robbie was improved. She sat at his bedside, holding his hand in hers never leaving him. As the second evening approached, Jenny knew she needed more help than that given by the doctors.

"Flo, go to the church and bring back whoever will come to pray," petitioned Jenny as the evening approached. "It's prayer meeting night and there should be some good people who will come in response to our call for help."

Before long the kitchen and parlor were filled with caring people with their heads bowed in prayer for Robbie's full and complete recovery. Throughout the night, fervent prayer crescendoed heavenward for the boy with people coming and going as they felt led.

Robbie made it through the night. Jenny was told that he now had a chance, but that his lungs were very weak and he had not regained full consciousness.

It was then that Jenny remembered how much Robbie wanted to study playing the violin. The memory of his determined little face the morning he had spoken to her about the lessons now haunted her. How she wished she had taken more time with his desire to play the violin.

"Brownie, do you remember telling us about a violin teacher who lived not too far from here?" Jenny asked as the kindly man brought her a cup of tea.

"Yes, I do," replied Brownie. "He lives a couple of blocks away."

"I just got to thinking," stated Jenny thoughtfully, "what if we asked him to come here and play the violin for Robbie. Perhaps it might bring him around. It might inspire him to fight and recover from his illness."

"Well, it couldn't hurt anything," concluded Brownie in agreement."

"What are you two talking about," asked Niki stepping up behind them as they spoke in soft voices near Robbie's bed.

"Jenny had an idea and it might be a good one," said Brownie, explaining what Jenny proposed.

"Oh, I don't know," worried Niki. "Maybe it would be too much excitement for the boy. He is so weak. Niki remembered well the hurt she had felt losing her child and could not bare the thought of anything happening to Robbie. He had become a son to her and Brownie.

She consulted with Martha and Benjamin who both felt it was an excellent idea. Within the hour, Benjamin and Brownie had found and convinced Professor Grant to come and play for the very sick child who lay so still and white upon his bed.

Soon, melodious strains of the purest music flowed from the strings of an old violin that Robbie so longed to hear.

Slowly, the boy began to respond. His eyelashes fluttered and he slowly opened his eyes, adjusting them to the light as the music filled the room. A faint smile crossed his drawn face and color began to show in his cheeks.

"Robbie," said Jenny, "Professor Grant has come to play for you."

"Oh, it is so beautiful," whispered the small weak voice as he half–smiled at the professor.

The sweet music continued a little longer, but Robbie had fallen asleep with a smile of contentment on his countenance. Soon after his fever broke and from that point on Robbie began to recover from his illness.

Each after noon for the next several days, Professor Grant came and played for Robbie.

The doctors were amazed at the healing process evidenced by Robbie's full recovery. Soon Robbie was able to sit up in a chair and before long, he was up and about. He was not yet well enough to return to school that term, but Jenny made sure Robbie began taking violin lessons. She was forever thankful that she had granted his desire to play the violin as the small boys' fascination for the instrument would someday thrill audiences around the world with his virtuosity for many years to come.

Chapter Thirteen

Jenny had not given a thought to the Valentine's Ball. In fact, it was the farthest thing from her mind. Robbie had been so ill and his slow convalescence had wiped it totally from her thoughts.

The bakery was going well again and things were getting back to some degree of normalcy. However, Robbie still needed a lot of attention and Elizabeth was still adjusting to being in school alone.

Jacqueline, sweet child, never tired of caring for her dear brother. He and Elizabeth shared so much and were always together, but now Jacqueline had Robbie to herself and she made the most of it.

"Wud Wobbie 'ike som mulk," she would ask him or "pillwo for your head?" Robbie's desires were her command and she would eagerly run and get whatever he wanted. She was delighted to wait on him in every way she could.

However, when Elizabeth returned from school each day, Jacqueline was happy to relinquish here role as all–around nurse and would attentively listen as Elizabeth related all that happened during the day with great care and detail not missing anything. Nothing was too small or trivial a detail that it couldn't be included.

Robbie had begun his violin lessons and the professor suggested it would be good if Elizabeth studied piano. Thus, the two could accompany each other and as Jenny knew nothing about music, they could help each other study. Professor Grant taught both instruments and would instruct each child once a week in the parlor after Elizabeth returned from school. Jacqueline would curl up in the big chair and listen in rapt devotion.

Jenny supervised the bakery and attended to the needs of the children. She carried a heavy load with all she had to do. Everything had progressed so well since their arrival in Boston but having almost lost Robbie she became less confident in her own abilities, a confidence she had gained during the first few months in Boston.

How she thanked God for answering prayer and Robbie seemed to get stronger every day. Still the situation seemed to have caused her to be burdened with a feeling of great uncertainty and loneliness, even when with her friends and family.

The nightmares, which seemed always with her now, increased with a vengeance. She silently suffered anxiety wondering what would become of her children if her mind were overtaken by the insanity of her dreams. Still, she remained outwardly calm and composed in the presence of everyone, but none would ever know or suspect the turmoil within Jenny's soul.

Martha grew apprehensive as the day of the ball was near at hand. She wondered if Jenny had totally forgotten about the Valentine's Ball, as she never mentioned it to her.

Finally, she could wait no longer. Details needed to be worked out and she so wanted Jenny to go. She could sense a sadness about her friend that had not been present before Robbie's illness. It would be good for Jenny and Martha did not want her to miss this opportunity to experience the splendor of the ball. It was with some reservation that she approached Jenny about this subject.

"Jenny," she began, "I am not sure if you remember, but we do have reservations for the Valentine Ball at the Gordon Mansion. Are—are you going to be able to attend?"

"I—I had all but dismissed it from my mind," answered Jenny with aloofness, "but, I suppose I can." Her former eager anticipation of attending the ball had given way to an indifference, but sufficient affirmation to inspire Martha.

"Oh, I am so glad," responded Martha, much relieved. "Your gown had been finished for sometime and I have just the right cloak for you and with enthusiasm she began to describe explicitly every intricate detail. It was made of rich black velvet with a white satin lining. She had purchased it in Paris but never wore it—explaining that she just didn't have the right occasion for its use.

"You are going to look so elegant, everyone will look with wonderment and the ladies envious at your appearance," observed Martha as if seeing Jenny in the gown. "However, I do wish you—well, I wish you would eat a little more in the next couple of days or else we may have to take the gown in more," she teased as she scrutinized Jenny with a shake of her head.

Jenny really had lost interest in the Gordons but was somewhat curious to see if there was any possible connection between them and her mother. That was her secret reason for attending the affair. Although, it didn't seem that important to her now, she had made a promise to Martha, knowing that she did not want to attend the ball alone, so she would honor her commitment which she had made before Robbie's illness.

The day of the ball dawned bright and sunny for February. The snow had almost melted away and with some imagination, you might be able to feel a touch of spring in the cool invigorating air.

Niki and Brownie insisted upon staying with Flo and the children the night of the party. They and the children were so looking forward to an evening together that it greatly relieved any reservations Jenny had about leaving them. It would be an evening of popcorn and long exciting stories of the sea.

At Martha's insistence, Jenny arrived at her friends' home late in the afternoon and was immediately whisked away to an upstairs room for any changes that had to be made to her gown. Her hair and nails were carefully groomed by servants who expertly performed their appointed duties. After that tea, tiny sandwiches and fruit were served in a sitting room before they dressed for the evening.

"I wish dear Benjamin could have joined us," stated Martha "but, you know he doesn't care a wit for this sort of thing. In fact this is the first time he ever really has shown any interest and I am sure I know why." Martha took a quick look at Jenny to see if she had caught the meaning of her words.

Jenny seemed oblivious to any meaning as she softly touched a locket dangling from a gold chain about her slender throat. Wanting to reinforce her desire to learn what she could of any possible relationship between Paulette and the Gordons, Jenny had taken the locket from its protected hiding place and fastened it about her neck.

"Why, Jenny, where did you ever get such an elegant piece of jewelry?" Martha asked, as she reached out and gently cradled the necklace in her hand.

"It was my mother's," Jenny said. "At least, I found it among her things."

"Jenny, this is truly beautiful," gasped Martha in disbelief as she held the locket still attached to the chain about Jenny's throat up to the light.

"It is of excellent quality. Where did she get it?" she questioned farther.

"I have no idea," replied Jenny slowly shaking her head.

"It is a perfectly lovely piece, one that would without a doubt complement any gown chosen for the ball. It think I am quite jealous," teased Martha, in a less serious tone of voice.

"Cora, come and help us with our gowns. Hurry now, or we will be late," called Martha, becoming acutely aware of the time.

The soft green dress was carefully pulled over Jenny's hair as not to mess it up and fastened around her tiny waist. When Jenny turned her lovely head with it's luxurious auburn hair and her ivory skin and looked into the full length of the mirror, it was like looking at someone she did not know.

"Oh, stammered, Martha, "you look so magnificent, you fairly take my breath away. You look like a princess or some sort of royal countess."

"I do look different, don't I?" said Jenny rather startled at her own appearance. "I think it's my hair, I have never worn it like this before," she stated while still examining the image before her in the mirror.

"Oh, Cora, where are our cloaks?" asked Martha turning with a smile which showed her dimples. Martha was someone who could turn a head also. She had tastefully chosen a mauve velvet with dainty white lace trim which offset her dark hair and olive skin. Her eyes were as brown as Jenny's were green.

Donning their long flowing cloaks the two friends set off for the ball just as the sun began to set in a red glow painting the sky with cascading brilliant colors.

It was difficult for Jenny to believe that she was really here, riding along the streets of Boston in a handsome carriage on the way to one of society's most plush affairs. Memories of life on the dismal farm seemed remote and distant and her terror of Jacque almost forgotten as her thoughts turned to the prospects of a most joyous evening. However, she could not help but feel some twinges of trepidation as the carriage approached their destination. Certainly, she was beautifully attired for such an occasion, thanks to Martha, but she did not feel the part inwardly. Would Boston's finest detect her charade and openly reveal who she really was? But, who was she? Staring into empty space Jenny felt the stark reality of it all—that she did not really know.

The carriage made its way along the darkening streets with the last rays of the sun fading into the night and silhouetting dark buildings and trees against the final red glow of the sky. Jenny wondered and hoped that Martha's gallant endeavors of instructing her in demeanor, etiquette and protocol for such a prominent occasion would not be forgotten as her nervousness and anxiety lay bare her ignorance of society's expectations.

Suddenly the carriage turned sharply, and they passed through high iron gates. It would seem that they had just arrived at the Gordon Estate.

"Is this it?" asked Jenny with her hands turning cold in her fine borrowed gloves.

"Yes, we are here," exclaimed Martha in delight. "Oh, look at all the carriages and people."

As she looked from the carriage, Jenny could see a long drive lighted with stately lamps all the way to the mansion. Many carriages lined the driveway.

The mansion was of massive structure, appearing suddenly out of the dark like a beacon showing the way. Lights seemed to blaze from every room. Music floated through the wide–open front doors greeting the guests with its melodic strains suitable for the occasion as guests were received in a constant flow.

"I—I think I know this place," murmured Jenny as she gazed about with a look of shock on her face.

"What did you say, Jenny?" asked Martha while gathering up her gloves and evening bag.

"I feel like I have seen this place before," returned Jenny, "It is like a dream."

"I know, we all dream of such a place as this, don't we?" laughed Martha. "Come now, we don't want to miss the Grand March."

Martha and Jenny took their turn in the waiting line inside of the grand foyer that led to the ballroom.

"Don't forget to give the doorman your invitation," whispered Martha in Jenny's ear.

"Alright," said Jenny softly but nervously being so totally occupied in awe of the grandeur of it all that she seemed unable to move her feet. However, Martha's subtle but definite urging jabs in her waist prompted her continued forward progress.

"Straight ahead," whispered Martha, "you have got to keep moving."

She could see into the ballroom now. A stairway wound upward across the other side of the immense marble floored room. It spiraled upward to the balcony which encompassed three sides of the upper floor and then continued to wind upward to a third balcony which duplicated the first. Colossal columns supported the lofty ceiling that was a tapestry of art. Crystal chandeliers hung in a radiating display of splendor adorned with sparkling pendants coruscating shafts of light.

Patrician ladies dressed in opulent gowns of flowing pastels accompanied by gentlemen suited in the sophisticated vogue of the period, graced the stairs and balconies as others glided across the ballroom floor in graceful movements synchronized to the melodies strains of a stringed orchestra.

"Announcing—Mademoiselle Victoria Forbes came a voice from a gentleman close to Jenny's side and Martha took the outstretched arm of a handsome young escort who whisked her away to an adjoining hall, now in view to Jenny, at the left of the ballroom.

"Announcing—Madame Jenny Lee Boshart," introduced the voice as Jenny briefly pondered on where "Lee" came from while being escorted by a charming young man in the direction Martha had previously taken. Now where did the announcer get "Lee" from...*of course...Martha...she made it up*, concluded Jenny to herself.

The hall was lavishly decorated with cupids and hearts; an ornate fountain filled with sparkling water was situated under a translucent glass domed ceiling revealing the partly visible moon and stars.

Long banquet tables were bountifully furnished with a variety of delectable foodstuffs and savory cuisine. Jenny strained to see—the lights were low in the great hall. The sound of orchestra music wafted through the room. Jenny began to feel twinges of pain pulsating through her head, but she was determined not to give in to its intrusion. Not tonight, Jenny told herself. All of this is not a dream, it is real. She felt like curtains in her mind were being pulled back and she could almost step into a different world.

"Jenny! Jenny!" summoned Martha's voice trying to get Jenny's attention.

"Yes—yes," responded Jenny slowly returning her thoughts to the present.

"The music has stopped and it is time for the Grand March into the ballroom," explained Martha in an excited but hushed voice. "Come and get in line with me."

Jenny's escort was patiently waiting to lead the lovely lady into the line that was quickly forming. She took his arm as the march began and followed him silently behind Martha and her escort.

The evening passed so quickly once the Grand March ended. Then they were swept into a slow gracefully beautiful waltz. After the waltz, they made their way up the majestic stairs and watched in fascination as a cotillion was perfectly performed by its participants. Then the lights were lowered and they sat on one of the marble steps, leaning against the rail as a troupe of ballet dancers suddenly appeared and entertained the guests on the dance floor below.

Martha stayed close beside Jenny all evening, introducing her to friends and encouraging Jenny to participate in the more simple rounds of music. Jenny would rather watch than take part so toward the latter part of the evening Martha, who was an excellent ballroom dancer, joined the performances at Jenny's insistence.

"Please, join your friends," coaxed Jenny, "I will be fine, we'll meet later in the great hall."

Jenny watched the symmetry of the dancers a little more then eventually found her way back to the great hall. She would entertain herself by looking about the lavish room filled with people. The stars had now come out and because the light in the hall was dim you could see them sparkling in the blue–black of the night sky high above the domed roof. Quietly she made her way through the throng of guests, laughing and talking—some with plates filled with exotic fruits and others with dainty desserts. The floors were made of solid granite covered with thick lush carpets. One of the walls was decorated with beautiful paintings, the genius of some renowned artists. Some were scenic landscapes of some famous places, some fascinating portrayals of still life, and then some portraits with unfamiliar faces.

However, Jenny stopped in front of one portrait of a woman partly obscured from her sight by the crowd of people between her and the portrait, and partly because of the dim light. It was also positioned high on the wall.

"I wish I could see it more closely," said Jenny to herself as she made her way closer to the picture. "Pardon me, please," she offered politely as she passed by those standing in the way.

There, she could see it more clearly now. There was something about that portrait in particular. She strained to see—yes, it was the lady in the locket. Just then, she felt a soft brush to her cheek and a strange overpowering need for her mother came rushing over her.

"Oh, Paulette!" she cried half aloud, "Why are you so entwined with soft and gentle memories of the past, and yet, never were you a part of them. What is wrong with me!" exclaimed Jenny holding her head with her hands. "I must be getting worse. I am afraid my nightmares are invading the reality of my life! Oh, how long before I become completely irrational and void of any sanity," speculated Jenny in silent terror.

She began to realize the seriousness of her seemingly abnormal behavior, and wondered if she should speak to Benjamin about providing for the children—to protect them should she... Then she felt secure in the thought that the Browns would take care of the children—she did not ever want them to fall prey to Jacques vengeful hands. Yes, as soon as Benjamin returned from New York she would set up an appointment and make the Browns their legal guardians—in case anything should happen to her. Thus, she dismissed these thoughts with a sigh of relief knowing the Browns would be willing to take upon themselves this responsibility.

"Jenny, Jenny!" called Martha, "I have been looking everywhere for you. Come, let us fill a plate with some more of this delicious food before they clear it all away for the evening and closing the doors leaving us shut out with nothing to eat. I'm suddenly famished again, aren't you?"

"I am a bit thirsty," responded Jenny, "and yes, food does sound rather inviting."

"Oh, I have had such a wonderful time," stated Martha as they each took a china plate and slowly began to move along one of the lavishly supplied tables.

"It is all so beautiful," commented Jenny, "so much more than I could ever had imagined."

"I so wanted you to have the opportunity at least once to see this place and experience somewhat its awesome panorama of luxury and charm," offered Martha. "It's just not easily described. I understand it was copied after a castle in Scotland where Rosetta was born and raised. Somewhere near Aberdeen.

Martha and Jenny continued moving down the length of the table taking small portions of the exquisitely prepared food. Suddenly Jenny felt herself being whirled around and in an effort to maintain her balance the delicate china plate fell to the floor. When she finally caught herself preventing a nasty and embarrassing fall she arose only to peer into the blood–shot eyes of Alex Gordon. In Jenny's bewildered state, she suddenly caught hold of Alex's jacket sleeve to steady herself. She gazed into his face and for a flash of a second she knew him—from somewhere– someplace—Oh, don't go, please, thoughts don't escape me now she pleaded within herself. Jenny stifled a scream from some emotion deep within.

"Yes, Yes! You are she," muttered Alex staring into her uplifted face. "Oh, Carrie…dear Carrie, you have come back to us."

In his drunken state, he stumbled and nearly fell, but his eyes became fixed on the locket and inadvertently reached for it almost in tender reverence.

"Assuredly, it is you," he whispered, but his grasp upon the frail chain was too much and it snapped, sending the locket dashing to the floor and disappearing into a crowd of people. Few in the crowd realized what had happened. Some of Alex's acquaintances that had witnessed his unpremeditated encounter with Jenny tried to help their unsteady friend from the hall, finding it somewhat amusing, since this was uncommon behavior for Alex.

"Leave me alone!" he yelled at them, flaying his arms about in the air until they had to grab him to keep him from falling and half carried him from the hall.

In the meantime, Jenny, with the aid of Martha, scurried about on the floor in the midst of the crowd in the area where the locket disappeared desperate to retrieve it.

Finally, after some time of frantic searching without any results except some trampled fingers and bruised knees, they decided it was useless to look any longer.

"Jenny, I am just sick about everything," said Martha as she put her arms about Jenny and hugged her tight. "Alex Gordon is the rudest person I have ever known and I don't know why he acted the way he did toward you."

"It was my fault," confessed Jenny, "I shouldn't have worn it. Perhaps it will be found if it hasn't been crushed under foot."

"Yes, Jenny," agreed Martha, "if we tell someone they may find it when the clean–up is done. We will leave word at the door and tomorrow I will make a special call my self on Rosetta Gordon and explain to her what happened. I want her to know how terrible Mr. Alex Gordon treated one of her guests—who happens to be my dearest friend. Come, Jenny, there is nothing more we can do tonight. The carriage has arrived, let's go home."

Jenny returned home without speaking hardly a word to Martha. Knowing how upset Jenny was Martha simply took her home and left stating that she would see her soon. Everyone in the house had retired when Jenny arrived and she quietly took advantage of it.

She was deeply troubled not only had she lost the locket that was her one link to Paulette's past, but also Alex Gordon had reacted to her in such a mystifying manner that it greatly perplexed her. Her own reaction to Alex upset her even more. She tried to rationalize what had happened to her. Some innermost thought, a fleeting memory, a glimpse of that face from the past—somewhere deep within a slowly illuminating dark corridor of her mind lay the answer. For an instant, Jenny had in bewildered awe seen into someone else's life—another place—another time. In that moment, she wanted to throw her arms about the person who had stood there calling her "Carrie."

"I am not well," she said softly to herself. "Perhaps if I could sleep." She changed from her beautiful dress into a sleeping gown and curling up on the couch, she tried to rest, but her head was racked with pain. "Jenny," she told herself, "You've come so far and conquered so much, you can't let this weakness overpower you now, especially for the sake of the children."

Then, as if driven by some inner voice, she slid to her knees and bowed her head.

"O, Lord," she prayed with great zeal, "I throw myself at your feet. Please, Lord help me! I don't know what is the matter with me. Since David and I prayed together some time ago and you became my Savior I have always believed that you would help me whenever I needed you, and you always have.

Earlier tonight was a happy time, but now the blackness swirls about me and I am afraid—I cannot breathe—please, Lord—help me to find a path out of this darkness, a way through this crippling fear."

For a moment, Jenny lay very still, then blinking open her tear filled eyes and focusing them in the moon lit room she felt that the pain had began to subside.

In her mind, she saw the mansion again as it had suddenly loomed out of the darkness as they approached it earlier that night. Shadowy images swept in and out of her thoughts as Jenny strained to recognize them. Yet, she was afraid that if she were able to connect it all together, the person she was would cease to be, and Jenny as she knew herself, would no longer exist.

Her sleep that night was broken and restless, with intermittent dreams of Alex Gordon walking and laughing together with a dark–haired woman and fleeting glimpses of a beautiful lady with hair the color of her own who bent down and kissed her sweetly.

Upon rising early, Jenny wasted no time—she was determined to make provision for the children's care in the event anything happened to her. Upon Benjamin's arrival home she went directly to his office where she explained in detail all she knew of her past, entreating him to begin a search as soon as possible into the identity of her mother Paulette and the vague memories she had of her early childhood. She divulged nothing about this to anyone else.

Chapter Fourteen

Rosetta Gordon wasn't at all pleased to hear that her son, Alex, had caused a scene in the great hall, especially when she learned he had been taken to his room in a drunken state.

She was summoned from the drawing room, where she had gathered privately with a few intimate friends. Rosetta had made her appearance at the ball earlier, but had grown tired and had withdrawn to her private quarters. The ball would go on well without her, and she would return toward the end of the evening and most would never have missed her.

As she followed the old servant along the hall toward Alex's room, she questioned him as to what had happened.

"I don't know, Mrs. Gordon, it seems young Mr. Gordon—well he became inebriated, if I might say so, madam, and he just wouldn't leave some lady alone. Some of his friends pulled him away from her, and by the time I arrived upon the scene, they were restraining him physically and then we—well—we escorted him to his room. We thought you should see him, as he is really disturbed about something, and we can't quiet him down. Perhaps we should send for the doctor," he suggested warily, knowing Mrs. Gordon was not one to take orders from anyone.

"Yes, Henry, that would probably be a good idea. Please return to the drawing room and see if Dr. Bennett has left yet. Hurry now!"

"Yes, madam," he said and then he scurried off in the direction of the drawing room.

Alex's friends had returned to the ball with the exception of two who had waited for Rosetta to come before they would leave him.

"Good evening, Mrs. Gordon, we are sorry to trouble you. We would have just put him to bed and let him sleep it off, however, he seems so agitated we were afraid that he might harm himself if we left him alone," explained Alex's friend as Rosetta entered the room.

"He seems quiet now," observed Rosetta looking at the troubled form of her son lying on his back on the bed fully clothed.

"What did he do?" questioned Rosetta.

"Well, we all had a few drinks of champagne throughout the evening, but you know, Alex rarely ever drinks, so I guess it was too much for him," explained his friend.

"I know," replied Rosetta with concern, "but it is during those rare occasions something like this happens. It is against my better judgment to serve champagne at these parties," she recanted as she began to take off Alex's shoes and loosen his tie.

"It was really strange, Mrs. Gordon, he just seemed to be drawn to that woman all evening. He became fascinated by her presence and couldn't stop commenting about her from the time she was announced. She was very attractive, and we all were rather taken with her. It wasn't until the ball was nearly over that I came upon the scuffle in the great hall and found him to be quite drunk and—well—making a fool of himself.

"I am sure it wasn't just the champagne," continued the friend further. "He kept calling her 'Carrie' to the embarrassment of the poor girl."

"Carrie! Carrie! Is that you?" mumbled Alex, as he sat up and then thrashed himself nearly off the bed, sliding toward the floor.

"No, no," calmed Rosetta, "I am not Carrie—now lie down before you injure yourself. The doctor is on his way."

"Is that you, mother?" he asked raising his hand to touch her as if to assure himself of her presence.

"Yes, it is I and you have had too much champagne," answered Rosetta. "You have made yourself ill."

"But," interrupted Alex excitedly, "She is here! Carrie is here! I touched her. She is alive and young after all these years," elucidated Alex as he tried to explain his encounter with the young lady.

"Alex, you are drunk—believe me, Carrie is not here," asserted Rosetta.

"Yes she is," groaned Alex as he tried to raise himself from the bed, "I want to talk to her *now*!"

"Dr. Bennett is here, Mrs. Gordon, so I will leave, but you see what I mean, he is very confused," stated the friend, still thinking it all rather amusing, but wishing no harm to come to Alex.

"I don't need a doctor," wailed Alex, "I don't want a doctor," and he fell back across the bed mumbling to himself.

"Charles," said Rosetta to Dr. Bennett, "can you give him something to calm him down?" as Henry with the help of Dr. Bennett moved Alex length ways of the bed.

"By the looks of him—I would say he has about had it. I think he will sleep now without anything if you can get him to lie still," suggested the doctor.

"Alex, you must be still so you can sleep," instructed Rosetta holding his hand as he began to thrash about again.

"She had Jenna's locket," muttered Alex staring up at Rosetta, "it fell to the floor of the great room."

"Try to sleep Alex, please" hushed Rosetta.

"I will, I will," he moaned, "but you must go to the hall at once. You must go now! It was Carrie, and she did wear the locket. Yes, it was she. It was Carrie.

"All right, shh, yes Alex," reassured Rosetta.

"Promise me," he whispered anxiously, "the locket—find it—it's somewhere on the floor of the great hall," he murmured.

Finally, he dropped off into a deep heavy sleep while Rosetta continued to sit with him long after the doctor had left.

Poor Alex, she knew what a burden he had carried all these years. Time had erased much of his memory, but there were times like these that everything seemed to come rolling back upon him. Rosetta had noticed that he seemed preoccupied lately, more so than usual.

Alex had for years now, been a model of respectability. He very rarely, if ever, dated, and the business had become his life. He maintained all that his father had left him, and with business acumen had increased the assets of Gordon Shipbuilding Enterprises, for which he sometimes traveled extensively.

Rosetta remained an active part of the business sometimes traveling around the world on company business with or without the companionship of her son. However, Alex did have many social acquaintances and on occasion was known to imbibe a little, much to his mother's distress.

"Dear, troubled Alex," whispered Rosetta to herself as she straightened the sheet and pushed his hair back off his forehead. He had suffered too much. Perhaps, she had not been fair to him. It was so hard to make the right decision. Perhaps, she had been wrong. He would probably sleep until late tomorrow, and she hoped all would be forgotten on a new day.

Still, as Rosetta started for her own room, knowing that the guests had departed some time ago, she wondered. Was it really the champagne that caused Alex to utter such incoherent gibberish, and witness what he so affirmatively stated he saw tonight? Being curious by nature, there were sufficient questions unanswered to warrant her inability to rest until she checked the great hall.

Summoning Henry, Rosetta asked him to accompany her to the now empty hall. Upon their arrival, they found a few servants still cleaning up and putting things in proper order.

"Did anyone find a locket while they were cleaning?" asked Rosetta.

No, they answered that they had not, but that they had been informed previously that there was one missing and that tomorrow a thorough search would be made.

"Henry, where approximately did the scuffle take place—do you remember?" questioned Rosetta.

"Well, let me see—oh, I think it was over here," explained Henry while trying to recall the events of the evening. "When they called for me to come they were by the table and Mr. Gordon was on the floor."

"Please turn up the lights, Henry," ordered Rosetta, "I want to take a closer look myself."

"Yes, madam, this is the spot right about in front of Miss Carrie's picture."

The light now turned high, brightly illuminated the face in the portrait. If Jenny had been there, she could have seen more clearly and recognized the portrait on the canvas as the same woman whose image was portrayed in the locket.

"Henry, bring a candle from the table. If there was a locket perhaps it rolled back by the wall where the light doesn't reach so well."

"There Henry, what is that?" asked Rosetta as the candlelight caught something shiny in its path.

"Why, I believe it is a locket, Mrs. Gordon," he said as he picked up the object and handed it to Rosetta.

As he placed it in her hand, Rosetta stared in unbelief. It was a locket for sure, and across the back was engraved the name *Gordon*. Alex's babblings were not just champagne–induced deliriums, but he had seen the locket, and here was the indisputable proof.

Rosetta tried to make her fingers move to open the locket, but she couldn't. It seemed to be authentic in its outer appearance—she caught the two sides of the locket between her shaky fingers and pulled it open, revealing Carrie and Jenna's likeness. This sudden astounding disclosure momentarily immobilized Rosetta, causing her to feel faint and seizing hold of the table, she tried to steady herself, but would have fallen if Henry had not caught her. She stood in a dazed silence, allowing Henry to support her. Henry broke the silence.

"It's them, isn't it Mrs. Gordon? It's Miss Carrie and Missie Jenna, after all these years," he stammered, "Where has it been?"

"I don't know, Henry, but Alex was right." Just then, Rosetta glanced up as the flickering candlelight caught Carrie's portrait, strange she hadn't noticed the faint smile before.

The next morning after much deliberation, Rosetta waited not so patiently for Alex to awake. She held the small locket in the palm of her hand and opening it carefully, scrutinized its contents. It was precise in every detail. There was no doubt in her mind that it was the same locket given to Jenna on her sixth birthday as a present from her mother, Carrie. Little information had been given to the public about the locket, if any. Holding it tenderly in the palm of her hand, she pondered sadly about where it may have been all those years, and who was the mysterious woman who was wearing it last night. Rosetta had not seen her. Tears filled her eyes as she meditated on the possibility that Jenna was still alive. She could not believe this to be true. It must be a cruel hoax, or perhaps some sort of extortion plan. Well, she would soon find out just what was going on.

Alex awoke very late. He awoke sullen and uncommunicative. Rosetta decided not to question him about the events of the night before while he was still in his present state of mind.

He drank some coffee and mumbled something about work that had to be taken care of at the office and left the house.

Alex had been gone only a few minutes when Martha, true to her promise to Jenny, arrived at the door. Rosetta received her in the library. Under ordinary circumstances, she would have been pleased to see the granddaughter of her dear friend, but today she had much on her mind.

"Would you please sit down, Martha," she graciously offered gesturing to a seat opposite her, "This is certainly a surprise. It has been so long since you have come to call."

"Yes, it has been, Mrs. Gordon and I should apologize for not visiting more often," acknowledged Martha.

"Martha, when did the granddaughter of my dearest friend decide to be so—formal as to call me, Mrs. Gordon?" admonished Rosetta kindly. "I am Rosetta to all my friends, and I would much prefer you to call me by my given name."

They exchanged pleasantries for a few moments, and then Martha changed the mood of the conversation.

"I have come to you with a bit of a problem," said Martha. "And because you are the dear friend of my deceased grandmother, I felt I could take the liberty of bringing it to your attention. I would not have mentioned it to you, but for our friendship."

"Why, what is it Martha?" inquired the concerned older woman. "I will do whatever I can to help. Now, what ever is your problem?"

"Well, it really isn't my problem," answered Martha. "It has to do with Alex."

"Alex?" repeated Rosetta in surprise, "Why whatever do you mean?"

"It seems that he has decided to treat a close friend of mine in a most tasteless manner. He caused her all kinds of embarrassment last night at the party, and previously, was very rude to her on another occasion when we were dining out together."

"It was your friend that the problem arose over last night?" asked Rosetta with a questioning look.

"Yes, she is a dear person and there should not have been any problem. She certainly did nothing to cause it, and I feel Alex owes here a personal apology, and..." but before she could finish Rosetta interrupted her.

"How well do you know this person?" questioned Rosetta.

"Very well, and she is a lovely person—a widow with three small children—working very hard to support them. She manages a small bakery just off Charles Street. She is a wonderful mother. I had a difficult time persuading her to attend the ball with me last night, as she goes out so rarely, and then Alex had to spoil it all."

"How long have you known her?" asked Rosetta.

"I have known her for several months now," replied Martha, "almost since her arrival here in Boston."

"She is not from the Boston area then?" inquired Rosetta.

Martha was becoming somewhat irritated at Rosetta's questions since, after all, she had come only to demand an apology from Alex and put an end to this nonsense. Did Rosetta feel that if Jenny's background did not come up to her social status that Alex's behavior was acceptable?

"No," stated Martha, "I believe she is from St. Louis, Missouri.

"I am sorry," offered Rosetta sensing Martha's sudden coolness, "I don't mean to imply in anyway that Alex's conduct was acceptable. I am very simply trying to piece together why he reacted in such a rude manner toward this woman."

Martha calmed a little at Rosetta's words.

"Perhaps it would help if I knew something about her, and you knowing her as well as you seem to, I thought you might be able to throw some light on this situation," continued Rosseta.

"Well, I would like to help, but Jenny is positive she does not know Alex. She has only lived in Boston since last August. She is not of the Social Register, but she is one of the finest people I have ever known. I admire her and her sweet children so much. I am truly angry at Alex for upsetting her and causing her to lose her precious and valuable locket."

"You call her, Jenny?" inquired Rosetta.

"That is her name," said Martha, "Jenny Boshart."

Rosetta fell silent as if in deep thought for a moment.

"Alex was very upset," stated Rosetta directing her gaze at Martha. I realize that he was also quite under the influence of champagne, which upset me a great deal. As you know, I have never condoned the use of strong drink of any kind. It is Alex who insists upon it being served in some degree at these social affairs. However, I am not totally convinced that was the only reason for Alex's distress. Believe me, there is no intent on my part to dishonor your friend in any way," continued Rosetta, "but any information you could give me about her background might be of a great help to me."

"I can understand a little of what you feel," replied Martha softening some, "but as much as I admire Jenny, I really know little about her before her arrival in Boston."

"Do you know if she has family anywhere?" inquired Rosetta.

"No, she has never mentioned anyone," answered Martha thoughtfully.

Her annoyance at Rosetta's persistent and personal questions about Jenny now caused Martha to stand to her feet.

"Somehow, Rosetta," exploded Martha, "I do not feel comfortable with this conversation any longer. I only came to declare my disappointment of Alex's display of rudeness toward my dear friend. Her personal background is her own affair and I have no reason to question her integrity."

Rosetta had hoped for more answers to questions she still wanted to ask, but realizing she had profoundly disturbed Martha, she politely offered her apologies.

"I appreciate what you have told me and I know it was only done with the kindest of intents," said Rosetta. "Please tell your friend we will reimburse her for the cost of the necklace."

Rosetta watched from the library window as Martha made her way down the walk and into the waiting carriage. Martha was such a nice girl, attractive too. Rosetta remembered sometime ago when Alex had shown some interest in her. If only Alex could forget and forgive himself. Yes, a small dinner party with a few close friends might be just what Alex needed just now. She would invite Martha and Benjamin, and a small intimate group of young people.

Chapter Fifteen

Rosetta finally moved from the window where she had stood for some time in deep thought. Yes, she mused, Alex had suffered much for his simple act of carelessness, perhaps too long.

After giving some instructions to be carried out by Henry, Rosetta ordered her carriage to pick her up, she had things to do.

Her first order of business was with her attorney with whom she had no prior appointment, but that made no difference to Rosetta.

"Well, good day," greeted the gentleman as she was ushered into his private office. "How can I be of service to you?"

"It would seem we have a problem," stated Rosetta as she seated herself with her usual commanding aura of authority.

"I am sorry to hear that," he replied with concern. "What kind of problem, Rosetta?"

"As you know, it has been a long time since anyone has come forth with any information about the disappearance of my granddaughter," she began.

"Yes, that is true," agreed the attorney.

"I am not sure if you remember," related Rosetta, "but there was a locket involved. The child was wearing it the day she was abducted."

"Yes, I do recall something about a locket," he reflected, "but I would have to pull the file for details though."

"Don't bother, just take my word for it," affirmed Rosetta, "there was a locket."

"Now, after nearly twenty years," declared Rosetta curiously while leaning forward in her chair, "it has been returned to us by way of a most unusual incident."

"In what way?" he asked now leaning forward himself with renewed interest.

"Around the neck of a mysterious woman who must re-semble my daughter–in–law enough to have upset Alex," lamented Rosetta. "Someone brought her to the ball the other night. In fact the person who invited her is a sister to young Benjamin Forbes, whom, I understand, has recently begun his law practice in these very suite of offices."

"Yes, that is true, Rosetta, but do go on," he prompted.

"Well, Alex had a little too much champagne at the ball," continued Rosetta, "and got into some sort of scuffle with the woman wearing the locket. Somehow, the chain holding the locket broke and the locket was nearly lost on the floor of the grand hall off from the ball room."

Rosetta stopped speaking and set back into her chair.

"Yes, yes, Rosetta, what then?" he urged her to continue.

"It's the same locket, I believe it to be the exact one that my little granddaughter wore that fateful day so long ago when she disappeared," concluded Rosetta with solemn regard, as she now handed the locket to him across the desk. "I have not seen the woman in question myself," confessed Rosetta. "But, I am sure it is some kind of extortion plot. It wouldn't be too difficult to find a young woman to pretend to be Jenna. Someone approximately the age she would now be if she had lived. Perhaps someone found the locket after all these years— Oh, why can't they just leave us alone." She bowed her head almost in tears.

"I am sorry, Rosetta," offered the attorney compassion-ately as he rose and came around his desk to pat Rosetta affectionately on the arm. He had been the Gordon's private attorney for many years now although he was not their legal counsel at the time of the child's abduction. However, he was a close friend, and fond of the Gordons. Therefore, he was very touched by the dear lady's remorse.

"We will do all we can to help," he said kindly still softly patting her on the arm as a comforting gesture.

"Yes, yes, please do, I want you to begin an immediate investigation of this woman," declared Rosetta gaining her composure. I will give you all the information I have about her and, of course, the cost is of absolutely no concern to me.

Please handle this immediately, but tastefully, we have had enough scandal already."

"We will begin today," he assured her. "Rosetta," he continued with great concern, "you and Alex could be in great danger—these people will stop at nothing to get what they want as you well know."

"Yes, and we will take utmost precautions," she replied beginning to perceive the seriousness of the situation.

Feeling much more in control now of the predicament with which she was confronted, Rosetta left her attorney's office and gave instructions for her driver to take her to the nearest telegraph office from which she sent a hurried wire.

"Return home now! (stop) Make haste! (stop) Rosetta Gordon.

The following morning came with clouds hanging low and the promise of rain. It was much too soon for any information to have been secured from the investigation just initiated. Still, Rosetta didn't feel like waiting idly by without trying to do something. Perhaps she would make a call on the woman herself, that way she could see what resemblance, if any, there was between this stranger and Carrie. Alex had already left early, stating he was meeting someone for lunch, so Rosetta, convinced that it was the right thing to do, donned a rain cape and soon was on her way. She would try a little investigating of her own.

"Driver, please stop at this address on the way," she instructed.

They had only proceeded a short distance when the carriage stopped in front of the desired address.

"Wait for me," said Rosetta hurriedly, "I won't be long."

She hastened up the walk through the light rain, trying the front door and finding it unlocked she went inside. Upon entering, she moved from room to room, giving out orders and asking questions at the same time. Why weren't there more men on the job, and how long would it take, were some of the questions she threw out to the workers. Then finding things somewhat to her satisfaction, Rosetta left as quickly as she came. Upon entering the carriage, she again gave orders to the driver to proceed as she continued her quest of locating the bakery. Martha had mentioned the name of the street, which wasn't too difficult to find. It took a short while and upon arriving, she again ordered her driver to stop and wait for her return.

She entered the front door over which read *Jenny's Bakery*, in large bold lettering, proudly hung there by Brownie.

There were several customers waiting by the counter making their selections, and small tables around which sat customers conversing and enjoying their tea and pastries.

It was quite unlike Rosetta, but for a moment, she hardly knew what to do. But she had come here for a definite purpose and soon she stepped to the counter and tried to feign interest in making a choice of bread to purchase.

"Could I help you with something?" sounded the rough voice of Brownie from behind the counter. He had taken it upon himself to help today, giving Niki some much needed time of work on the books.

"I think I would like a loaf of the wheat bread," answered Rosetta, "and, oh, yes a dozen of the sugar cookies." She wondered who this person was, and where was the woman she had come to see.

"Yes, madam, and we have fresh sugar cookies comin' from the kitchen right now. Elizabeth, sweetheart, hurry with the cookies will you, mate?" he called to someone in the back room.

In a moment, a door swung open from a hallway behind the counter and a fresh aroma of baked goods flowed in with a little girl carrying a try full of cookies.

Rosetta looked up with an incredulous look upon her face. The child appeared like an apparition from the past. Exactly resembling the one lost so long ago.

"Here, Uncle Brownie," smiled the little girl. "Flo said to tell you they would have been done sooner, but Jacqueline spilled the sugar all over the floor and they had to go and get more. Jacqueline is really in trouble today." Just then, a large, bright colored ball came rolling through the open door, with a small child right behind. The ball rolled around the counter and stopped by Rosetta's feet.

"My ball," laughed a sparkly–eyed child as she ran into the room to retrieve it.

Rosetta was still staring at Elizabeth in awestruck disbelief. Then she glanced down at the small child at her feet looking up at her with a mischievous grin.

"Hel–wo," smiled Jacqueline innocently as she bent her chubby little body to pick up her ball.

"Oh, Jacqueline, you know you are not to play with your ball in the house," came the stern, but tender voice of a young woman who now appeared from the kitchen area. She moved around the counter and picked up the child, ball and all.

"I am very sorry," she apologized to Rosetta. "Did the ball strike you?" she questioned. "Jacqueline is bored, she has had to play inside because of the rain today."

Rosetta took one look at Jenny and realized why Alex thought he had seen a ghost. The similarity was quite breathtaking to say the least. This woman certainly bore a great resemblance to Carrie. The hair eyes—yes, even her soft mannerisms. It was uncanny. Rosetta, always so in control felt she was completely losing her poise.

"I do hope you are not hurt," questioned Jenny further, not having received any reply from the lady who stood staring unabashed at her.

"Hurt? NO—No, I am not hurt," said Rosetta picking up the baked goods as she suddenly turned and dashed from the bakery to her waiting carriage.

"I hope she is all right," said Jenny, still holding Jacqueline and looking somewhat bewildered as she watched the lady disappear into her carriage and head down the street.

"Well, how do you like that?" remarked Brownie shaking his head in disgust. She never paid for the baked goods. It sure wasn't 'cause she couldn't afford 'em. Did you see her carriage, and the jewelry she had on? She scooted out of here like she was being chased or something," he rambled on.

"Never mind, Brownie," said Jenny, "I'm sure she just forgot. It was rather strange, though, I mean the way she stared at me and for some reason she seemed kind of familiar."

"Oh, ya, well—maybe, you met her at that fancy party you and Martha went to," suggested Brownie with a shrug, still showing his annoyance at what had happened.

"Perhaps," answered Jenny thoughtfully, "that could be."

The incident at the bakery was soon forgotten. Jenny spent much of her time with Robbie who was still recovering from his illness. He appeared stronger day by day as summer drew near. His ardor for the violin had not diminished and he practiced with such intensity that Jenny was concerned he would tire himself. Somehow, the more he practiced the greater his energy as if he were being transported into a realm of enchantment that was beyond her understanding.

Elizabeth far and beyond what anyone might have assumed was impressive in her own right, displaying exceptional skill on the piano. The amusing side of her personality sometimes caused her to be judged as less of a scholar than her brother. That was proven to be untrue. Elizabeth, who had come to Boston with little schooling, had taken honors for achievement at the close of the spring session. Her devotion to Robbie was ever present and that intuitive sense that flowed between them formed an inseparable partnership in their music throughout the coming years.

School had now ended for the summer months. It was a warm Saturday afternoon, the weekend before the Fourth of July. Robbie had gone to spend the day with Brownie on one of the trawlers; the fresh warm sea air would be good for him. Niki had left early to do some shopping and had taken Elizabeth and Jacqueline along with her.

Flo had just placed the last trays of baked goods in the front counter of the bakery.

"It looks like we can close early—we are almost sold out," observed Jenny. "Maybe you and I can sit out on the back porch where it is cool and relax for a few minutes before we start supper."

"That would be a most welcomed relief," smiled Flo. It had been warm in the kitchen all day.

They both looked up as the little bell jingled over the front door and Benjamin entered looking quite concerned.

"Hello, Ben, coffee's on, would you like some?" asked Flo.

"Thank you, Flo—but not right now. I really need to speak to you about something, Jenny," he stated in a serious tone of voice.

"Something wrong?" asked Jenny, "Is Martha all right?"

"Martha is fine, but something has come up that I need to discuss with you," he answered trying to get to the reason for his visit.

"Well, no one is home, but come on into the parlor," said Jenny as she motioned for him to proceed through the open parlor door. Leading the way, Jenny directed him down the hall into the comfortable chamber. It was warm, but there was a nice breeze blowing into the room through the open screened windows. The bright sun gave a bright pleasant glow to the room. She closed the double doors to the hallway and walked over and shut the kitchen door. It wasn't that she cared if Flo heard the conversation, but certainly didn't want anyone else to hear.

"Jenny," he began as he seated himself atop the round piano stool, "perhaps you had better sit down."

"You have found out something then—something about my mother's past?" faltered Jenny as she felt for the chair behind her.

"Some—not too much," he answered, "not too much about your mother—more of your husband Jacque."

Then, standing up from his seated position on the piano stool, he slowly walked across the room to stare out the front window away from Jenny's gaze. He was silently endeavoring to collect his thoughts to properly word what he had to say when he was interrupted by Jenny.

"Ben, I asked you to find out anything you could about my mother—my past—whatever you have found out I need to know," declared Jenny beseechingly. She remained seated on the chair waiting eagerly for Benjamin to reply.

He turned around and looked at her with a troubled frown.

"Jenny, I had to secure information about you in order to trace your mother," he explained. "My sources have revealed to me that your husband was deeply involved in various crimes. He is wanted for armed robbery and he may have been involved in an international group that is highly secretive. Who they are, and what are they planning, we do not know. Your husband is wanted under several aliases. The man you were supposed to be espoused to is a noted violent criminal.

"Supposed to be married to," interrupted Jenny with indignation as she arose quickly from her chair. "What do you mean?" she questioned.

"Jacque has a wife and children in France that he never bothered to divorce before he married you," he explained.

"I—I can't believe that," mumbled Jenny, "why—why would he do such a thing?"

"We are not sure, but Jenny," he continued, "there is some question by the authorities as to what implication you may have had in this whole affair. Right now, they do not know if you are alive or dead."

Jenny reeling under the devastating blow of what had been disclosed to her about Jacque, seemed numb to the idea of her being involved in any way.

"I have no knowledge of anything Jacque has or has not done," related Jenny. "But why would anyone think I was dead?" she asked, suddenly realizing what he had said.

"Jacque is apparently dead, Jenny—he drowned in the Kaw River a year ago. Because of the devastation in the area caused by the flooding river, his body was not found for sometime. He was finally identified by the contents of his wallet. Some neighbors buried him in the vicinity of your farm. The farm was completely washed away, and no one knew for certain what happened to you and the children."

"Jacque is dead?" Jenny gasped in astonishment.

"It would seem so," answered Benjamin.

"Jenny," continued Benjamin after a few moments. "The authorities do not know where you are or what, if anything, has happened to you. I know that you had nothing to do with any of those awful things that Jacque was involved with. Please trust me, and I will help you all that I can." Benjamin tried to be comforting, but looked as devastated as Jenny felt. He was, without question, in love with her. How it grieved his heart to see her look so dejected.

"I do trust you, Ben, and I am grateful that you believe that I could not be a part of any of Jacque's crimes," she confided softly.

"As far as any data on your mother," explained Ben, "we have not been very successful. She emigrated from a small town in France about two years before she took the position in St. Louis. We found from her immigration papers that she arrived in New York City with a sister by the name of 'Monet'."

Producing a small notebook, he proceeded to read some of the details that he had jotted down.

"The two sisters took up with a traveling troupe of entertainers—dancing, acting, etc. When they arrived in St. Louis Paulette stayed there, no longer continuing with the troupe. Neither Paulette, nor her sister, Monet, were accompanied by any children when they arrived in the states."

"Did you know your mother's sister?" interjected Ben.

"No—I don't remember her," answered Jenny after some thought.

"You probably speak French though," reasoned Ben.

"Very little," she replied, "I can recognize the language when I hear it, but I cannot read or speak it with any fluency. Paulette left some letters written in French. They were concealed in the secret compartment of her box, along with the necklace, but I cannot read them."

Suddenly she remembered something like a flash before her eyes. "Benjamin, I think the name 'Monet' is signed on those letters," blurted Jenny excitedly.

"Where are they, Jenny?" asked Benjamin with great interest. "Can you get them for me?"

"Yes, yes," she answered, "wait here, I'll be right back."

Jenny hurried to her room and quickly took the wooden box from a drawer. Yes, the letters were there along with a picture that she had forgotten.

Returning to the parlor, she gave Benjamin the letters and picture.

"Do you know the women in this picture?" he questioned, holding up the photograph for her to see.

"I believe this one to be Paulette when she was younger," related Jenny pointing to the woman on the right, "I do not know the other woman."

"Jenny," counseled Ben with a look of great concern, "please try not to worry. Believe me when I say that I have competent and reliable individuals pursuing every lead we can find. We will soon discover how Paulette came to have the locket in her secret possession and where she acquired it. I had to come and explain what information has been obtained so far. Perhaps these letters will shed some light on all of this. Do you mind if I take them and the picture with me? I don't read French and I need to take them to someone who can translate them for me."

"Yes, take them, Ben," agreed Jenny, "they are of no use to me. I pray that they will lead to something positive, something definite that will clear everything up."

She attempted to assure Ben that she would not worry, but it was quite useless. She stood alone in the still room as Ben left closing the double–doors to the hallway behind him. Remorse flooded in upon her as she allowed her grief to surface. Jacque was dead. She had never thought it would end this way. The abrupt finality of a life—it was all so tragic—so unexplainable. Silently she wept, alone, confused—caught in a tangle of webs that was not of her doing.

Chapter Sixteen

The strange little man had seemed to appear from out of nowhere once again. Jenny noticed him when she was walking Elizabeth home form school one day in the late spring. He was walking behind them at some distance when she glanced back.

"What is it?" Elizabeth had asked as she caught her mother nervously looking over her shoulder.

"Nothing I guess," Jenny had replied, taking Elizabeth's hand in a firm grip and picking up their pace.

"Is that man following us?" Elizabeth had questioned, stating that he was the same man who has been standing out by the side yard of the school lately.

"I guess he likes to watch us kids play."

Upon hearing that, Jenny had been relieved that school was nearly over. Perhaps, she had thought, he lived nearby and meant no harm. However, she had taken a detour down a side street, hoping he would not follow them. It had appeared he did not.

She hadn't seen him again until he came into the bakery. Jenny had brought a fresh tray of bread from the kitchen and he was seated at one of the little tables having a cup of tea. She was sure it was the salesman they had met in Sedalia – the same one Elizabeth had collided with at the rail station. He peered over the rim of his cup with a beady stare. Jenny almost dropped the tray as she felt the penetrating coldness of his squinted eyes leveled at her. He stared intently at her as she placed the loaves of warm bread on the shelves of the glass counter. She hurried back to the kitchen and when she returned a short time later—he was gone.

The weekend before the Fourth of July had been especially busy. Flo had commented that everyone in Boston must have needed baked goods. They doubled all their baking efforts and it seemed there wasn't a minute they were not rushed. Martha even came over to help, allowing herself to be pulled away from whatever seemed to be keeping her so occupied this summer.

Robbie had become somewhat of a regular on Brownie's trawler and Brownie, who had been extra busy with a good haul of fish, was not able to assist at the bakery. The salty air worked like a tonic on Robbie and he seemed to have regained some of his strength.

There had been a parade and celebration on the Fourth with fireworks following in the evening. The Browns, Jenny and the children, Flo, Martha, and Ben all gathered together for a picnic in the park.

The fireworks display was spectacular and everyone agreed it was the best they had ever seen. Following the fireworks display, Brownie and Robbie headed back to the fishing boat to bunk on the trawler that night. It would give them an early start in the morning.

"Don't forget your fiddle, Lad," Brownie reminded Robbie as they bid goodbye to everyone for the evening. The boy liked to practice as he sat long hours on the boat watching the fishermen haul in their nets and enjoying the seascape. The men grew to enjoy the sweet violin music as it floated melodiously across the water.

Jenny saw the pudgy salesman again on the trolley as they boarded it that night for home. They were in a jovial mood and he seemed to pay them no attention on the short ride to their stop. He remained on the car when they exited at their destination, so she dismissed it from her mind.

Elizabeth and Jacqueline went straight to bed with Flo following soon after. Jenny and Niki sat for a time talking in the kitchen where a cool breeze was blowing in through the back screen door.

Suddenly a noise in the back yard stopped Niki in the middle of her conversation.

"What was that?" she asked startled as she arose and went to the door. She opened the door and stepped out onto the porch.

"Do you see anything?" asked Jenny as she followed her onto the porch.

"No," said Niki peering into the darkness, "I guess it must have been a cat. Probably knocked something over on the other side of that fence," she decided.

Returning to the kitchen, they closed and locked the door behind them.

"I sure hate to close off that nice breeze," said Jenny, "but, there are a lot of strangers still on the street from the festivities of the holiday, and I feel safer with the door closed and bolted."

"That's all right," replied Niki. "I am so tired, I could sleep in a furnace tonight, besides, there is a nice breeze blowing from the windows in your room.

Niki was sure she would be perfectly comfortable in Robbie's room across the hall, and the two retired for the night.

Sometime before dawn, Jenny sat bolt upright, jolted from her sleep by the sound of breaking glass. Before she could place her feet into her slippers and reach for her robe, the unmistakable smell of smoke permeated the room, activating her sense of danger. With her mind racing, she pulled Jacqueline from the bed and woke Elizabeth. It was so dark, she could not see. The smell of smoke grew stronger. Clutching her arm, she pulled Elizabeth toward the hallway. She could not see into the room occupied by Niki, and she did not respond to Jenny's screams. The smoke was so heavy, that it was with great difficulty that she fought her way through the parlor and down the front hall.

"Flo—Flo—get up—the house in on fire," she shouted in terror up the stairway to Flo's apartment.

Flo had already been awakened by Jenny's screams and was half–way down the stairs, when Jenny threw open the door to the front court yard and they all fairly tumbled and staggered into the fresh night air.

"Where is Niki?" wailed Flo in alarm.

"I don't know," gasped Jenny as she inhaled short breaths of air. "She—she must still be inside the house. Watch the children, don't trust them to anyone. I'm going back inside to find her."

She disappeared into the dark of the smoke filled hallways before Flo could attempt to stop her. The smoke was now so heavy she could not get back down the hallway to the parlor. She thrust open the side door into the bakery attempting to cross from the bakery and reach the kitchen. Inching her way blindly reaching for tables and chairs to guide her she stumbled and nearly fell as she heard a low moan from across the room. Dropping to her knees, she hugged the floor, inching her way forward. The density of the smoke made it all but impossible for her to see the still form lying on the floor in front of her. Jenny stumbled and fell over Niki's unconscious body lying on the floor.

"Niki! Niki is that you?" choked Jenny with her own lungs nearly bursting for air. A low moan came from Niki's lips as Jenny struggled to pull Niki toward the area of the front door. She could see the flames in the kitchen area engulfing everything in its way. The door seemed to be ajar and now someone thrust open the door and helped drag Niki's limp body from the doorway to the safety of the outside.

Some late night celebrators had come upon the fire and ran to alert the Fire Station that was only a block or two away. The horse drawn engines came clanging down the street as Jenny fought to bring Niki back to life.

"Niki," sobbed Jenny, still choking from the smoke filled air her lungs had received as she cradled the semi–conscious head of her friend in her lap. She felt something wet and sticky on the palms of her hands.

"Blood!" agonized Jenny, "Her head is bleeding. Oh, what happened to you, Niki?" she pleaded as if to receive some response from her languid friend.

"Jenny—Jenny—is that you?" questioned Niki in a faint and faltering voice.

"Yes, yes!" answered Jenny. "Oh, dear Niki—what happened? Can you tell me?"

Just then, Flo and the girls joined them from the side courtyard. There was no gate in the courtyard fence and someone had broken down a section of the iron fence to let them out. Flo attempted to comfort the frightened children as Jenny continued her efforts to revive Niki.

By that time, the building was engulfed in flames, and as the fire horses trotted in with the fire engines, everyone was forced to move away further down the street to greater safety.

Niki was carried with care a safer distance from the fire by a robust young gentleman. He explained to Jenny that as he and some of his friends had passed by on their way home from a party they had seen a man run from the front door of the bakery and hurry down the street. They thought it was somewhat unusual but continued on for a few moments when one of them looked back and saw the smoke. Not realizing the bakery was inhabited, they had gone for help, returning just in time to help Jenny pull Niki through the door.

"Jenny," mumbled Niki as she tried now to speak. "The front door—someone—broke the glass and I—I went to see—I thought it might be—Brownie."

"Yes, I heard the glass break too," soothed Jenny trying to comfort Niki.

"The lady needs a doctor," said the young man in a worried tone, "we should get her to the nearest hospital."

"I'll get a carriage," blurted an authoritative voice as an uniformed officer took charge.

"Jenny," whispered Niki so weak it was hard to hear her as Jenny bent down to help place Niki in the carriage. "Someone was in the bakery—I saw him—He was in the kitchen—when I turned around someone struck me from behind—oh—my head aches so...."

"I understand, Niki," said Jenny trying to calm the distraught friend. "It will be all right—lie still—we will follow you to the hospital as soon as we can."

The carriage then sped off in great haste into the night.

Looking dejectedly at the smoldering ruins of what was once a thriving bakery business and comfortable home; Jenny realized that there was nothing she could do. Everything seemed lost to the flames and smoke.

She left an account of her whereabouts with the authorities and then realized to her dismay that all her possessions had perished in the fire.

"Flo, we don't even have coins for a trolley," anguished Jenny.

"Yes, we do," revealed Flo," holding up a small purse. "I grabbed my purse on the way down the stairs."

"You are an angel," declared Jenny giving Flo a big hug. They stood together the two women and little girls in the dawning light of morning, only in their besmirched nightclothes reeking of smoke.

"Flo, dear, could you take a trolley and escort the children to the Forbes' home across town?" requested Jenny. "Please explain to them what has happened. I believe they will offer us some assistance. Would you also ask Martha to bring me a change of clothes. I must go immediately to Niki at the hospital."

"Of course I can do that," consented Flo as she put an arm around each of the little girls. "Oh, there comes a trolley now."

They began to run and reached the trolley stop just in time. Jenny watched them speed away with the little girls weaving frantically from the window of the departing vehicle. Jenny caught the next car headed in the direction of the hospital and ignored the amused 'once–overs' and snickers of the few morning frequenters. She was in such a state of distress that she hardly thought of what she was wearing.

In fact, her thoughts were so profound that she missed her stop and as the conductor called out a street name she suddenly dashed from the car and had to rush back nearly a block—her long robe tangling annoyingly about her ankles.

"Please be seated in the waiting room," instructed a nurse in a starched white gown.

"But—I need to know how Mrs. Brown is," explained Jenny anxiously.

"The doctor is with her now. We will call you as soon as he is finished," answered the nurse.

Jenny tried to wait calmly, but she seemed to have little patience for sitting and she was pacing back and forth across the room when Martha and Ben found her a short time later.

Martha had brought her some articles of clothing in a smart little bag and Jenny immediately hurried off to change.

She soon returned looking much more suitably dressed in spite of the clothes being two sizes too large for her.

The Forbes assured her that Flo and the girls were fine and they had left them taking some breakfast and resting comfortably in the care of their faithful servants.

Just then, a man dressed in a doctor's white frock entered the waiting room.

"Mrs. Boshart?" he inquired.

"Yes, I am Mrs. Boshart," answered Jenny with a solicitous look in her eyes.

"From what we can determine, Mrs. Brown has had a rather severe blow to the back of her head," he explained. "We had to use several stitches to close the wound. She is experiencing some dizziness now. We feel it would be best to keep her here under observation for awhile. She is also suffering from some smoke inhalation. As soon as she is admitted to her room, a nurse will come for you. She is anxious to speak with you."

The doctor then left stating he would see her again tomorrow.

Jenny was soon shown into Niki's room and quickly went to her friend's side, taking her hand in her hands as Niki attempted to explain what had happened, but it was difficult for her to talk.

"Jenny—you will need a place to stay," she said weakly. "Brownie and Robbie will be home tonight. Take the children and you and Flo, and go to my home near the wharf. We have two extra bedrooms. They are small, but you will be safe there with Brownie."

"That sounds like a good idea," said Jenny, "But, please try to rest now."

"First, I must tell you—someone set that fire, Jenny—I saw them," asserted Niki. "There was a little man standing by the door. I saw his face in the light from the fire. He wore glasses and had a pudgy face. I tried to run for help, then I felt a sharp blow to the back of my head.

"Oh, Niki, you could have been killed! I'm so sorry," conveyed Jenny slowly shaking her head in disbelief and thoughtfully adding, "It's beyond my conception as to why anyone would do such an awful thing."

"Don't worry about me—they will take good care of me," said Niki, feeling relieved and somewhat exhausted, but noticing Jenny dressed in other than her night attire added with a smile, "How did you get a change of clothes?"

"Martha and Benjamin are here," explained Jenny. "They are in the waiting room now and are most concerned for you. Martha brought me a change of clothes. Flo and the children are safe at the Forbe's home."

When Jenny returned to the waiting room she found a police officer speaking with Benjamin and Martha.

Seeing Jenny enter the room he approached her and began to ask some questions as to what had happened for his report. Jenny divulged what little she knew and what Niki had told her.

"It definitely was arson, Mrs. Boshart," affirmed the officer, "I am afraid there is nothing valuable left. The fire is contained but still burning. Do you have any idea who would want to do you harm?" he questioned.

Jenny assured him that she had no idea as to why anyone would wish to do them harm.

Chapter Seventeen

Rosetta Gordon was not a patient person. Neither was she one to grovel over her mistakes. That morning, she was radiant, having, with gratification, concluded a promise she had made a long time ago, and with much greater satisfaction than she had expected.

Alex looked so happy when he had left the house that morning. He even hummed a little tune as he waited for his carriage. Business seemed to keep him away a great deal of late; still he had never appeared so serene.

Rosetta remained in the sunny comfort of the breakfast room after Alex departed. Ordinarily, she would have finished reading the morning paper over a cup of tea, but this morning she was in a reflective mood. Instead, she gazed with deliberation out across the spacious well–kept garden. Droplets of the morning dew clung to the flower petals and blades of grass and shrubs sparkled like tiny diamonds as they caught the suns bright rays. She sat with her shoulders straight and her head held high. Her demeanor was commanding, and even at the age of seventy–three, she was strikingly imposing. Her snow–white hair was stylishly coiffured, and her manner of dress was flawless in every detail. She was of medium height, and extremely trim, having always been meticulous about her appearance. Her thoughts now were on Alex and the past.

James, Sr., would have been so proud to see how Alex had turned his life around completely from the irresponsible young man he had once been. Rosetta continued reminiscing with a feeling of nostalgia, the events of those earlier years.

She and James, Sr., had met near her home in Aberdeen, Scotland at a county fair. Although strongly opposed by her father, who felt James was much below her station in life, eventually, after some time, the couple was allowed to marry. In the year 1850, immediately after a grand wedding, James had taken his beautiful young bride and sailed for Boston to secure Rosetta's dowry, a small, ill–run ship building company given to them by her father. Dedication, hard work, and God's favor prospered the little company into a diversified multi–million dollar enterprise.

They were euphoric when James, Jr. was born in 1853, and again almost six years later, when Alexander arrived to multiply their blessings.

True, Rosetta had probably indulged Alex too much, but he was a loving child and such a charmer. James, Jr. was his father's child, equally good–looking, but of a more serious nature. The two boys were raised with strict Scottish principles, and received the finest schooling and education money could buy. James, Jr. followed in his father's footsteps with a dedication to the business that was fervent and dauntless. Alexander on the other hand loved the fast life.

Alex met Carrie at a garden party given by some mutual friends. She was seventeen and her appearance was delicate and lovely. Her auburn tresses complimented her ivory complexion. She spoke with a soft Irish accent, having emigrated from Londonderry only a short time before with her father, who had taken a position teaching at Harvard. Alexander was completely taken with her beauty and demeanor. He fell in love with a beautiful young lady, in a garden filled with flowers whose fragrance enhanced a moment captured in time. For her, he would change his life around. He began to seriously court Carrie throughout the summer months, but then she met James, Jr. Although he was eight years older than she, the chemistry between them was perfect, and it was to be a lifetime commitment for both of them. James, Jr. and Carrie were married in the spring just after her eighteenth birthday.

Oh, how Alex had brooded. He had always been allured by fast living, and was easy prey to loose women and alcohol, but he excused himself, not to weakness of character, but to a broken heart. He left the business primarily up to his father and older brother as he indulged himself in hedonistic pleasure.

Time erased the memory of what might have been, and he finally accepted Carrie as his sister–in–law. When Jenna came to grace the Gordon's household, he loved her as his own.

Although Jenna was pampered by her grandparents, and to some she may have seemed spoiled, she was a contented and joyously happy child. She knew nothing of sadness or grief. Her life was the focal center of family life where all was happiness and comfort and where everyone willingly catered to her every whim. She was idolized by her 'grandpapa' and 'grandmama'—names of endearment by which she called her dear grandparents. She adored her Mama and Papa, and they adored her; but it was Uncle Lixie, as she called Alex, who was the love of her life. Lixie never refused her anything. He worshipped the child. She was highly intelligent and just as pretty as her Irish mother, inheriting her natural flawless beauty and auburn hair. She was witty and charming, and the world was her domain until that dreadful August afternoon when it all came crashing down. Rosetta shuddered at the thought of it. Alex had repeated the events so many times.

Every Thursday afternoon of that summer, Carrie let Alex escort his little niece to the park. She so looked forward to it, even though Carrie had some reservations. Alex did not often meet with approval, and he knew it. After their excursion in the park, Alex always took Jenna home with him to the Gordon Mansion for dinner and to spend the night with her doting grandparents.

Rosetta recalled how her beautiful grandchild loved the mansion, and how they lavished her with their affection. The child's wishes took priority over everything. Her laughter and exuberance rang through the hallways, and the many rooms bringing the place alive with her spirited childish joy.

She loved to have Grandmama make the music box in the ballroom play, as she and Uncle Alex danced about in great swirls and sweeps across the empty ballroom floor. Rosetta smiled as she could hear the childish "look Grandpapa—look Grandmama, how pretty the lights are." and hear her laugh in glee throwing back her head of long auburn curls to watch the sparkling chandelier as she and Lixie whirled about to the enjoyment of everyone.

"How short those precious evenings," sighed Rosetta. It seemed as if she could almost feel the soft touch of her granddaughter's cheek nestled against her own as finally the child gave in to fall asleep on grandmama's lap.

"Mama will come in the morning," the little girl would always whisper just as she drifted off to sleep, "Mama will come in the morning."

The presence of Jenna and Alex in the park on Thursday became common knowledge, as the two would stroll down the many paths mutually enjoying each others' company, as they rode on the park's swan boats in the calm waters of the lagoon and fed the stately snow white swans.

A short time before that fateful afternoon, Alex had met Monet at a party. She was an actress, newly arrived from Paris. She sang and danced for their entertainment, and became very attracted to Alex. He thought her interesting and quite seductive. She certainly wasn't his type, he thought, but he wouldn't mind seeing her again.

Carrie had cautioned Alex not to let Jenna out of his sight, for she was becoming difficult to keep up with at times. She knew her little girl would not hear of missing the afternoon with her fun loving, handsome uncle, but that day, Carrie had an uneasy feeling

"Let's go, Lixie," coaxed the child, pulling him by the hand.

"Bye, Mama," she said as if to dismiss her mother, "we'll see you tomorrow."

"Give mama a kiss," said Carrie, bending and giving the little girl a hug and kiss.

"Please be careful," Carrie had cautioned Alex again. "Perhaps I should go with you."

Jenna coyly whispered in Carrie's ear that Lixie would feel bad if she did.

"All right then, I'll see you in the morning," said Carrie as the child and her adoring Uncle

Lixie walked away hand in hand.

The child turned and looked back, her sweet face graced with childish innocence. She lifted her free hand again and blew a kiss toward her mother.

"I'll see you in the morning," she returned and blew another kiss. "I'll see you in the morning."

They had a delightful time feeding the ducks and swans, Jenna riding the pony after which they sipped some lemonade. The best of all came when they boarded the unique swan boats for a boat ride.

As they approached the pond, suddenly the temptress, Monet, appeared as if by a quirk of fate. She smiled seductively at Alex as she approached the two of them, and with flattering words, 'oohed' and 'aahed' over Alex and the adorable child with him.

"Come on, Lixie," demanded Jenna while pulling on his arm toward another direction, and showing her dislike for the unwelcomed stranger.

Alex was overwhelmed by the lavishly painted, black–eyed Monet.

"I—I am coming," he said hesitantly while looking intently at Monet.

"But—Lixie—the boat is ready to go," she had coaxed while pulling on his sleeve.

"Just a minute," he said gently while stalling for time.

"No, Lixie!" pouted the little girl, stamping her dainty white shoe in impatience. She wasn't accustomed to waiting for what she wanted. "I want to go now!" she demanded.

Monet was making her move on Alex with all of her coquettish charm. She would like to take a walk for some lemonade; she coaxed Alex while referring to him as 'Mon Cheri,' smiling all the while.

"I can take the little girl around the pond," spoke up the boat tender. "Take the pretty lady for a walk and we will be back in a few minutes. I will take good care of her," he assured Alex.

Alex was completely infatuated by the alluring Monet, and although he had second thoughts about allowing Jenna out of his sight, the boat tender seemed trustworthy, and he had been there all summer and Jenna was impatient—so it was agreed.

Lixie lifted the delighted child high into the air, her white dress flowing and billowing in the soft breeze as he swung her laughing into the boat.

"We'll be right back, Lixie—now you be good," she giggled pleased she was having her way.

Alex watched them slowly ply their way over the smooth surface of the pond while another Swan Boat pulled up to dock.

Monet took Alex's arm squeezing it amorously and as they strolled along the path, she captivated him with her flirtatious comments and her beguiling French charm.

They slowly made their way up the hill to the lemonade stand with Alex keeping an eye on the little boat and pond. They lingered over the cool sweet lemonade while speaking to each other intimately.

After a few moments, Monet abruptly excused herself, thanking him for their brief interlude and the lemonade, and left with promises of seeing him again soon.

Alex returned to the dock to wait for Jenna, but neither the boat nor Jenna appeared. It was found some time later as Alex searched hysterically for the young child. There was some evidence of a struggle, and blood was found on the seat of the boat.

Alex was beside himself as he wildly imagined the spectrum of gruesome possibilities.

When it was evident that the child could not be found, Alex resigned himself to the heart rendering task of disclosing to the family what had happened.

Initially, Carrie could hardly grasp what Alex was saying. But sudden realization of it all manifested itself in a feeling of horrifying grief that spontaneously soon erupted into a fierce anger toward Alex, vented by calling him every despicable name she cold think of while screaming uncontrollably.

"Why did I ever trust you with my baby? I despise you—you destroy everything beautiful that you touch—you have destroyed my life.

A letter for ransom arrived before morning demanding a tremendous amount of money. It was to be paid at a location many miles from Boston. James, Jr. was to deliver the money, small denominations—used not new bills, at a designated time and place. According to the note that was explicit in every detail, there was to be no deviation from the instructions. The authorities were not to be contacted, and if they followed the note exactly, Jenna would be safely returned.

On the prescribed day, everything, as far as the family knew, was being carried out exactly as they were instructed by the note. However, James, Sr., feeling that without the help of the authorities they may never see his precious granddaughter again, arranged for the police to become involved in the process.

Jenna's Pa–Pa left the ransom just as he was told, and then turned and walked to his carriage some distance away, not looking back to where he had placed the money. But, before he could leave the scene, shots rang out. He waited anxiously for some report of what had happened. He was later told that the police had shot and killed the extortionist when he had fired on them.

As previously assumed, it was the trusted boat tender. If he had any accomplices, they were never found. He seemed to have emerged from nowhere as their investigations revealed no past, no friends and no family. There was no apparent link between him and the flirtatious Monet who had vanished without any trace.

Jenna did not come home.

The Gordon family utilizing all the resources at their command searched in vain. James, Sr. condemned himself for the disastrous part he had played, Alex was inconsolable—not being able to forgive himself for his carelessness, and Carrie blaming them both, but with her vindictive hostility focused on Alex, also shared the guilt for not obeying her premonition. Rosetta and James, Jr., tried to console them in their grief while with aching hearts they tried to return some sense of order to the family life.

The child had disappeared without a trace. It was rumored that she had been murdered by her abductors and was buried in some unknown grave.

The search continued for many years with false leads and shattered hopes. The case was never really formally closed, but the search finally diminished through the years due to the lack of any new clues.

Carrie never forgave Alex for the part he played in the loss of her beloved Jenna. She refused to speak to him again and he was not allowed in her home.

After some time had passed, James, Jr., took his wife on a trip around the world on a company owned steamer, leaving their painful memories and futile efforts far behind them. However, they would never forget their precious little girl.

But, tragedy again would force its way into the Gordon's household. The ship sank during a typhoon spawned by the monsoons off the coast of Malaysia. It was reported that the ship had capsized during the storm and they were never found.

Before they left on their combined business and pleasure trip, Carrie had forgiven James, Sr., realizing eventually that he had made a mistake in judgment—fearful for his granddaughters life, but not meaning to jeopardize her safe return.

Weakened by years of remorse and unsuccessful searching for his granddaughter, the stress and strain upon his aged mortal body finally took its toll. Rosetta's dearly beloved James, Sr., passed away.

Alex had changed completely. He had truly loved Carrie, and when she spurned him for his brother, it hurt him profoundly, but when she turned against him in disgust of what he was, he could no longer stand himself.

He loved Jenna deeply, as though she were his own. The tragic circumstances of her disappearance became the catalyst that completely transformed his former contemptible life. He began to take an active part in the business, putting aside his carousing antics. He ardently continued his pursuit of some information about Jenna. He traveled many hundreds of miles in vain attempts to find her.

He was a strong support for his older brother, James, Jr., who had forgiven him, knowing Alex had not meant any harm to come to the child. He cared for his mother with devotion and when his father passed away, he zealously committed himself to the family business with great deftness and ability. His personal life became almost extinct, very rarely dating anyone and when not traveling for or preoccupied with company business lived a rather solitary life in the great mansion with his mother.

Alex was well liked and respected. The most eligible young ladies on the social register sought after him relentlessly. He received many invitations to various social functions, but accepted few and although gracious to a fault, he never gave any indication of serious intentions toward any other woman. For in his secret heart he carried a picture of a young and beautiful red headed girl clearly seen in his mind's eye in a garden filled with fresh and lovely blossoms.

If things could have been different—if she hadn't hated him so much—if she could have given him some comforting hope to his tormented mind by forgiving him—then, perhaps— he could find release and go on with his life. How he despised himself for what he allowed to happen, the awful grief he had caused. Dear sweet Jenna gone—only God knew where, and Carrie and James both vanishing into a watery grave.

Rosetta, herself, had remained resilient and indomitable throughout the years. I came from stubborn Scottish heritage, she would say, and we never give up. Adversity only serves to strengthen and fortify our resolve.

And, yet, with all her tenacity and strength of character, there were times when in a solitary place, grief would open the door to her emotions and allow a brief moment of being overcome by a longing for the truth—of what had really happened to her dear little granddaughter.

Oh, how she longed to see beyond the veil of uncertainty and know what had happened on that dreadful day.

Chapter Eighteen

Jenna had gleefully boarded the little Swan Boat that fateful day and had scowled a disapproving glance back at Lexie for deserting her for that bad looking lady. She would certainly tell Grandmama when she arrived home, and then Lixie would be in real big trouble with everyone.

For now, she would enjoy the ride. How she loved it. She rested her petite hands on her tiny lap in the folds of her white frock relishing the ride as they glided across the smooth surface of the water. She loved the feel of the softness of her dress as her childish mind drifted off into happy thoughts.

"Someday, very soon, now, Grandpapa and Papa were going to take her on one of their own big ships, maybe—way far across the sea. Maybe this very year, as they had promised."

She put her head back and looked up at the azure blue sky with its white billowing clouds all puffed up and forming various recognizable images. Jenna glanced down to see two white swans propelling themselves gracefully past the boat. She would have been able to feed them if Lixie had come as he always brought bread crumbs with which to feed them. Maybe Lixie would take her around the pond again when he returned, that is if he didn't want her to tell Grandmama about the painted bad lady.

Oh, what was that she wondered as the boat bumped into the side of the embankment and threw her against the side of the boat.

"Don't you know how to steer?" she questioned the boat tender sternly while trying to support herself due to the slanted position of the boat.

He didn't answer her; instead, he jumped into the shallow muddy water and with haste roughly hauled the craft up and into the bulrushes along the shore, bumping the fragile child about.

"What are you doing?" she shouted in fear and anger.

"Shut up! Shut up! You brat," the man snarled threateningly.

Now, fearing that her life may be in jeopardy she tried to climb out over the side of the boat.

"Lexie! Lixie! —Help me please," she yelled, but no one heard her screams for help.

Then, suddenly with a final lunge the muscular tender jerked the boat forward into a more secluded hiding place. All Jenna could see was blue sky and white billowy clouds as her head was propelled backwards. That lunge had sent her flying back striking her head against the sharp edge of the wooden boat seat. With a sharp 'bang' all became blackness. There she lay, still and motionless, her eyes open and staring into space, blood flowing profusely from the wound in her head onto her soft white dress.

"Oh, I have killed her," moaned the gruff tender as he stared in disbelief at the still form of the young child.

Quickly, he produced a large thick sack and picking up the bloody child, shoved her into the pouch. Then grabbing it around the top, he threw it over his shoulder and hiked out of the park through and over the overgrown ditch that flowed into the pond. Not very far outside of the park he came up under a bridge and waited, while glancing nervously around and up towards the road. Soon a horse drawn buggy raced upon the bridge and stopped abruptly. A woman jumped down from the buggy seat and called to someone under the bridge.

"Where are you?" she called softly in an uneasy voice.

"Here I am," answered a husky voice out of the darkness followed by the accomplice making his way up the small incline toward the road. He climbed quickly into the buggy, dropping the bundle in the place beside him on the floor. Then grabbing Monet by the hand quickly pulled her into the carriage, and with one swift simultaneous motion and shaking of the reins, had the horses trotting into a full gallop. Looking at the bundle lying still on the floor she looked at the rough looking partner next to her and questioned him concerning the little girl.

"She isn't moving. Is she all right?" questioned Monet.

"I don't know, I think—she may be dead," he answered solemnly looking at the still form of a small body in the sack.

"Oh, you stupid fool! What have you done?" Then grabbing his sleeve roughly she wailed, "We will be hunted down as murderers!"

"It was an accident," growled her partner as he jerked his arm from her grasp and prodded the horses to go faster.

In a quick matter of time, they were headed out of Boston and into the countryside.

Monet quickly untied the sack and gently pulled the bloodied child from its confines.

"I need some water," she fumed while trying to waken Jenna by slapping her ashen face.

"What do you think I am—crazy? We cannot stop now," he shouted back at his distraught companion.

It seemed like hours before they finally turned off onto an old dirt road that gradually merged with a trail through the woods, ending at a ramshackle old building.

Jenna drifted in and out of consciousness.

Quickly, the tender lifted the young child from the carriage and brought her inside as Monet lit a lamp. Putting her on the rough wooden floor, he started to leave.

"I must go now if our plan is to work," he stated as he headed for the door.

"What? You will leave me all alone in this forsaken place with a dying child. I will not stay!" cried Monet as she closely followed him to the door.

"You will do exactly as planned if you value your life," he snarled, while turning abruptly and grabbing Monet roughly by the arms. "I could snap your skinny little neck right now. You are of no real value to me anyway."

"When will you be back?" questioned Monet changing the tone of her voice now fearful for her own life.

"If I am not back at the appointed time agreed upon, take this brat and hurry to our next destination. I will meet you there. There is a horse and wagon in the shed out back."

Monet waited by the door for a brief moment, and then returned to tend to Jenna. The child became more alert as time passed and she could finally sit up. Dazed and confused she began to sip some water from a cup held to her lips by Monet. However, she remained dull and unresponsive to her name when spoken to her by Monet.

When her fellow conspirator did not return at the proper time, alone and frightened, Monet prepared to take Jenny to their next destination.

Taking some scissors from her bag, she cut Jenna's long auburn curls, clipping her hair short. Then she dressed the frail child in boy's clothing, and after bandaging the deep wound on the back of the child's head, pulled a cap down over her hair.

Then Monet changed her own appearance—donning an overly padded dress and covering her hair with a blond wig.

She needed to hurry, in order to reach the small town nearby, and make connections with the train that would carry them to New York City.

Jenna gave her no trouble. Monet carried her onto the train and placed her in a seat in one of the passenger cars. The child rode in mute silence.

Once in the city, Monet proceeded in the direction of the hotel where she was to meet her partner. She waited uneasy and uncertain, apprehensive as to why her partner had not yet come. Picking up the newspaper that was delivered to her door, she soon discovered that her partner had been shot and killed as he endeavored to collect the ransom. Suddenly realizing the dilemma she was in—she became jittery and agitated. Her only thought was to take the child and leave as soon as possible.

Sometime later, in the middle of the night, Monet pounded on the door of the upstairs living quarters over a tavern in St. Louis, Missouri.

"Who is it?" retorted the sound of a woman's rough voice from the other side.

"I need to speak to Paulette," said Monet anxiously.

"It's three o'clock in the morning and we are closed. Go away," voiced the sleepy reply. "Come back tomorrow."

"No, you fool. Go and get Paulette and open the door," demanded Monet.

"Oh, all right, just a minute," acquiesced the voice as the sound of footsteps faded away down the hall behind the door.

In a few minutes Paulette, half asleep, opened the door.

"Who is it and what do you want?" she yawned while rubbing her sleepy eyes.

"Paulette, it is me, Monet, your sister, let me in," she blurted out as she pushed her way through the open door pulling Jenna unsteadily behind her.

"Monet, what are you doing here and why are you dressed like that?" questioned Paulette staring unbelievingly at the plump blond with Monet's voice.

"Never mind, I need your help and I am in a great hurry. Where is your room?" she asked searchingly while looking about. "I must speak to you with complete privacy."

Paulette led the way to her room and shut the door.

"Lock it," demanded Monet motioning toward the door.

"Oh, don't be so ridiculous," scoffed Paulette while at the same time obeying her command.

"Paulette," said Monet speaking in a hushed tone. I am in great trouble. It's a long story, but I want you to keep the girl for a short time. I will come back for her, but I cannot keep her with me at this time. It would be most dangerous for me."

"Monet, what have you done?" demanded Paulette sharply.

"Shh," cautioned Monet putting her fingers to her lips.

"An acquaintance and I stole the child. She is from a very wealthy family, but things did not go as planned."

"But, that is a boy," stammered Paulette staring at the small quiet child.

"No, she is not. We had to disguise her," explained Monet in a distressful tone. It was evident she keenly felt the turmoil she was experiencing.

"Well, what do you expect me to do?" questioned Paulette in disgust and beginning to feel used and drawn unwillingly into Monet's mysterious web of unlawful activity.

"I want you to keep her until things quiet down. Then I will work out a plan for her return. You will be very rich, Paulette. I just need time to work things out," explained Monet.

"What about your friend?" asked Paulette.

"He's dead—killed by the police at the site where the ransom was delivered. But, Paulette, I do not believe they even suspect me or know where I am. We were most careful not to ever be seen together," explained Monet.

Seeing that here sister was beginning to become intrigued by the idea Monet introduced the prospect of great monetary gain.

"Paulette, there may be millions involved here. We could live in luxury for the rest of our lives instead of you slaving away in this dingy bar and me traveling about with some tawdry acting group. It may take a while, but I have a plan," she added.

"Oh, yes," said Paulette with increasing interest.

"Yes, Paulette, and I promise it will not take too long before I return and put my plan into action," stated Monet.

"But, how do I explain her to the others?" questioned Paulette gesturing her hand toward the hallway.

"Well, let me see—tell them she is yours," said Monet.

"Mine?" exclaimed Paulette, raising her voice in disbelief.

"Shh, quiet," warned Monet, then after a brief moment, "Yes, you see, she has had a bad bump to the head. It was an accident, but she cannot remember anything. She is what you would call, disoriented."

"But what if she remembers?" asked Paulette while looking at the confused child.

"We will cross that bridge, if we come to it, but right now the only thing she has said so far is ma–ma. She has asked for her several times so I told her I would take her to her Mama and here you are," said Monet with an amused smile.

"You are sick," returned Paulette with a grin.

We will see when the money comes rolling in," laughed Monet with a smirk.

"Well, is it a deal or not? I am in a hurry," questioned Monet.

"I can't support a child," argued Paulette, "I can barely supply my own needs."

"Here," said Monet as she handed her a small tight wad of bills. There will be more very soon," she added with confidence.

"All right," Paulette said with hesitation while adding, "you had better be right about this." Then looking at the child she asked, "What is her name?"

"Just call her Jenny," stated Monet while standing and starting to leave. Then, remembering the object in her hand she turned to Paulette.

"Oh, I almost forgot," she said. "Here, this is very important. Put it in a safe hiding place away from everyone." Then she handed Paulette a shiny expensive looking locket.

"It was around her neck when we found her. It contains a picture of Jenny and her mother. Guard it with your life. It is the only proof we have of who she really is."

True, it was somewhat of a surprise the next morning when Paulette presented Jenny as her daughter, explaining that she had left her in the care of a family member who could no longer care for her. The questionable character and environment of the 'establishment' was such that no one really questioned or cared or ever disputed the fact that Jenny was Paulette's child.

Jenny's hair eventually grew long and lovely again covering the scar on the back of her head.

Monet wrote the first year, sending periodically enough money to somewhat satisfy Paulette's selfish nature.

Over the next five years, she wrote only a few more times, sending enough money to keep Paulette interested, and always with the promise that she would come soon for Jenny. Then silence.

Paulette began to drink more and more, but always remained silent regarding Jenny, ever hopeful of rich rewards until the very day of her death when she turned the box over to the little girl who had so drastically interrupted her life so many years ago.

Monet had assumed that a quick return would have been negotiated for Jenny to her family. However, her intentions were as ill fated as she and her bungling partner's original plans. Neither of them were endowed with any extraordinary gift of intelligence, and their plans had been botched from the beginning to the end with incompetence and poorly initiated strategy.

After successfully placing the child in the keeping of Paulette, Monet fled to Quebec where over a period of time she involved herself in many illegal ventures. Still, at least once a year she faithfully sent Paulette enough money to keep here interested.

She wanted desperately to claim the ransom, but the fear of being found out, haunted her life. She fell ill and the ravages of tuberculoses claimed her life before she was able to succeed in her endeavor—ending all hopes of Jenna returning to her family.

Chapter Nineteen

He sat with his head down—his hands covering his face. Sobs shook his stocky frame as the bald headed little man wept aloud.

"I didn't mean to do it," he murmured over and over again. "Why, oh, why did that woman have to come up behind me," he whimpered to himself as he continued to lament his case.

"Mr. Braun, Mr. Braun," demanded someone standing over the distraught man. "Do you wish to make a statement?"

"I never meant to hurt anyone—I could have put the fire out if she hadn't startled me," he groaned.

"Mr. Braun, this is a police station. I understand you wish to make a confession. Is that true?" questioned the voice above him.

Max raised his head and looked up, searching the room as if not sure of his surroundings. He rubbed at his squinty eyes with one hand while holding his thick glasses with the other. He wet his lips nervously and twisted his pudgy body about trying to adjust to the chair.

"Yes, Yes, I do," he answered, "all I wanted to do was to find Jacque Boshart. I wanted to kill him."

"My name is Sergeant O'Rourke and I will be taking your statement," the officer informed Max Braun.

By this time, a clerk had been summoned to write down the words of the extremely troubled man's confession.

"You are admitting to arson of that bakery a couple of days ago over on Charles Street, is that right?" questioned the uniformed officer.

"Yes," sniffled Max, "but it was an accident—an unfortunate accident."

"Why did you do it?" prompted Sergeant O'Rourke trying to make some sense out of the situation.

"Why? Why, you ask? Because I wanted to find Jacque," responded Max wildly. "He doesn't deserve to live."

"Who is Jacque?" inquired the officer calmly realizing the unbalanced mental state of the man who sat before him.

"He needs to be found and punished – I have looked everywhere," said Max sobbing even more loudly than before. "Perhaps you would know where he is?" questioned Max hopefully looking up at the officer. "He is a wicked man, but I am through searching. It isn't right that innocent people should suffer for his wrongdoing. That is why I am turning myself in."

"Did you try to kill Jacque by burning the bakery?" asked the Sergeant.

"No, I just went there to search the place for information—as to where Jacque might be," explained Max, "My lighted match caught the kitchen curtains on fire."

"And you struck the lady over the head?" interrupted the sergeant.

"I didn't want to, but I must have panicked," stated Max Braun, "is she all right?" he added thoughtfully. "There were people coming—I could hear them. I had to get out of there—I ran and ran and when I looked back, the bakery was in flames. It was so horrible," he nervously recalled. "I really didn't mean to hurt the lady," he continued, "I was only trying to find a lead on Jacque. I've been hiding for two days too afraid to come out."

"Who is this Jacque and why did you want to kill him?" demanded the Sergeant realizing now that this man who identified himself as Max Braun was saner than he had first thought.

"Well," began Max, staring off into space as if reliving the events he was about to relate. "Some years ago that scoundrel, Jacque Boshart, came to work in the bank in the little town where I worked as the head bookkeeper. I was engaged to a sweet young girl by the name of Effie." Max stopped abruptly rubbing his forehead as if in deep thought.

"Please go on," coaxed the officer seeing how difficult it was for Max.

"Effie worked as a teller," continued Max, "folks said she was plain, but I thought she was pretty and nice you know," related Max with a smile of recognition on his face as he lovingly reflected on Effie.

Slowly he proceeded to tell his story.

"She was shy around most people but the two of us could just talk and talk and she made me feel that I wasn't common or alone anymore. When Jacque came along, he just changed her. He controls and manipulates people with his charm and good looks. It wasn't long after Jacque and Effie became friends that large sums of money were discovered missing from the bank. The books had been tampered with and suspicion fell on me. I was sure Jacque was influencing Effie and using her position as head teller to gain access to the bank vault. I just couldn't incriminate her—she was the victim—a young lamb being led to the slaughter." Then feeling the impact of Jacque's irresponsible and callous nature Max blurted out, "I wanted to kill him! I wanted to kill him."

"Mr. Braun, I know it's hard for you, but we need to get to your confession," stated the officer to the distraught figure before him. "That's what you are here for isn't that right?" he questioned.

"Yes, all right," agreed Max continuing with his story, "there was sufficient evidence produced to prove my guilt and I was sent to prison. Jacque and Effie disappeared. Finally, after serving my time I was released and began my search for Effie. I knew it wasn't her fault. I found her grave in a lonely and obscure cemetery. He used her for his purposes and discarded her as useless. I then went looking for Jacque and I have since that time been searching for him."

Max stopped here and inhaled a deep breath with an examining glance about him. He seemed to have become so lost in the past that it was difficult for him to adjust to his surroundings.

"Is that the end of your confession?" asked the officer, not quite sure if that was all.

"No," stated Max and continued, "I searched everywhere for him carrying a gun in my briefcase just waiting for the right moment to come. Then finally, I tracked him down. It was in St. Louis, Missouri. But illusive as always, Jacque suddenly disappeared with his wife and family. Then quite by luck I came upon Jacque's family at a boarding house in a small town in Missouri. I had seen Mrs. Boshart with Jacque in St. Louis before but I wasn't positive that this was she until I secretly checked the registry at the boarding house. Jenny Boshart was her name all right. I waited for Jacque to join them and when he didn't I followed them all the way to Boston, but I lost them."

Then shifting his position and quieting himself somewhat he continued, "I guess it was fate in a manner of speaking that caused me to discover one of the children playing in the school yard. I waited and sure enough, Mrs. Boshart came to escort her daughter home. I followed them right to the bakery. I closely watched the bakery for weeks hoping to see Jacque, but he didn't show up. I just couldn't wait any longer and I decided to search the living quarters to see if I could find any information that would lead me to Jacque."

Here Max ended his story and sat quietly with his head in his hands. He would accept his fate not caring about the consequences of his confession. What did he have to live for anyway? Nothing, all that mattered was gone.

It was several days later that Benjamin and Jenny came to the jail. Jenny had been told of Max's confession and Benjamin had attempted to find out if the despairing story Max related was true. It appeared what he said was factual. Max had spent nearly seven years in prison for embezzlement of bank funds. Finally, he was proven not guilty and set free. Max's Effie had perished as he said, left sick and alone to die an untimely death.

The meeting between Jenny and Max was an emotional one. She walked into the jail cell accompanied by Benjamin. Max sat in a solemn state. His demeanor as somber as the cheerless gray of the walls that held him prisoner.

"Mr. Braun," said Jenny gazing intently toward the grief stricken man sitting before her. "I am Jenny—Jenny Boshart," she explained.

Quietly she stood waiting for some response.

Slowly Max raised his head. He was not an attractive person. His appearance was drab and repugnant.

"Yes, what do you want?" he spoke gruffly yet with a break in his voice.

"I have come to see how you are," she spoke firmly staring directly at Max as she pondered as to what character this unusual person really was.

"Why would you do that?" he questioned squinting at her somewhat perplexed.

It seems that you have been put to a great deal of grief by my husband, Jacque Boshart," said Jenny plainly.

"It doesn't matter," whispered Max thoughtfully, "nothing matters."

The mental state of his dejection, was so consuming that Jenny reached out and laid her gloved hand on Max's shoulder as if to somehow console him.

He looked at her gentle hand placed so tenderly upon him and suddenly his body shook with sobs of regret. He threw himself on his knees and without looking up begged Jenny's forgiveness for all the grief he had caused her and her family and friends.

Jenny was quite overcome by Max's sincere manifestation of contrition.

"Mr. Braun," spoke Jenny softly, "Please, please get up. We forgive you and after hearing your story, I have a better understanding of the circumstances that brought you here."

"But, I nearly killed that woman," he moaned. "And the children could have perished in the flames. Oh, what have I done! Oh, what have I done!"

"Yes, what you did to Niki was a brutal attack, but I now understand it was done out of desperation," stated Jenny.

Slowly, Max stood to his feet coming eye to eye with Jenny who was short of stature. His face was etched with grief.

They spoke quietly for a few moments in the confines of that room. It was a brief but enlightening encounter between completely different individuals drawn together by the injustices done to them by one unprincipled profligate. In the short conversation that was exchanged Max Braun saw a Godly compassion in the young couple that stood before him. It was like a faint flicker of light that he had never witnessed before, but it grew in his spirit until it became his guiding light.

The consequences of what Max Braun did were costly and brought physical suffering to Jenny and the Browns. In spite of it all, it was decided that sending Max to jail would only damage him more. He never went back to prison—no charges were filed and Max left Boston never to return. From that time on, he took a new path, a new direction following a higher purpose for his life.

Chapter Twenty

The Brown's cozy home was nestled in amongst the long rows of houses built close to the wharf. It was convenient for Brownie who kept his trawlers moored just across the street. The house was comfortable and attractively maintained even to the bright pots of red geraniums that lined the colorful steps leading up to the front door.

Niki's recovery had been slower than first expected. It has been nearly two months, now, since the attack on her life and the fire. The blow to Niki's head had caused her to have severe headaches and had affected her left side with a slight paralysis. By following the doctor's prescribed exercising regimen the paralysis was now very minimal and the headaches much abated, but Brownie still did not want Niki left alone. He was positive they could find another suitable place for the bakery when Niki fully recovered.

Jenny, Flo, and the children had remained with the Brown's since the first day of the fire. Martha and Benjamin had hoped that they could persuade them to stay with them in their spacious home, but understood Jenny's desire to stay close to and help care for Niki.

In spite of the tragic course of events that had brought them to live with the Browns here along the waterfront, it had been a more pleasant summer than expected. Flo and the girls occupied a large upstairs bedroom with a breathtaking view of the ocean. Jenny had a small room on the main floor where she could be close to help with Niki if needed. Robbie slept on the parlor couch when he wasn't out on one of the fishing trawlers with Brownie. Niki's jovial personality transcended her affliction and made caring for her an easy task. Flo did most of the cooking while Jenny busied herself about the house and caring for the children.

At first, the children found great pleasure in just following Flo around the kitchen or listening to Niki and Jenny chat in the parlor. After a few days they found that there were many other children in the neighborhood and soon made many friends. They would play in the backyard or on the front steps all day in the warm sunny breezes blowing gently from off the water. By early September, they were tanned a golden brown and Jenny had never seen them look so robust and happy.

Whenever the trawlers were out to sea Robbie went along now. They hadn't experienced any bad weather days except for a couple of summer storms. Jenny worried about him, but he loved the water almost as much as the violin.

Robbie's reputation as a fiddle player had become quite well known along the docks and on the fishing vessels that summer. The violin was his constant companion and he practiced whenever he could. One evening as he and Brownie were sitting on the brightly painted front steps relaxing after a long haul on the trawler, Robbie picked up his violin and began to run through some of his exercises. The ethnic group of seafaring folk living along the water–front would congregate on their front steps listening to the lively tunes from Robbie's violin while enjoying the cool breezes wafting across the deep blue waters, catching the last rays of the fading sun. They would converse back and forth in their broken English as the day's events were passed along the wharf from one step to another.

Robbie wasn't sure anyone was really listening as he ran through some exercises and then moved on to a short piece he had learned. Even though it was a classical piece, when he had finished it was quiet along the wharf. Just as Flo and Jenny joined them, a voice rang out over the still hush.

"Can you play, 'O Solo Mi O'?"

All was still for a moment more. Then Brownie spoke up in a voice loud enough for all to hear. "I don't think he knows it. Hum it for him, or shut up."

The strapping Italian got up off his porch and made his way down the street, his heavy footsteps thudding against the stones under his thick boots. He stopped directly in front of Brownie's step. Brownie stood up straight with his hands tucked into his belt with a defiant look planted on his face. Then the muscular Italian in ethnic garb tossed the bright scarf loosely about his neck—throwing his dark curly hair back and sang with great gusto the requested Italian aria.

Robbie had rested his violin across his knee, while watching uneasily as the impressive figure of a man came down the street. Now, he quickly picked up his violin and placed it on his shoulder, tucking it under his delicate chin and began to play an accompanying melody. It took him a moment or two but soon he drew the bow across the strings of the violin, producing rich deep tones in exact melodious harmony with the Italian. By the time they had finished playing, Robbie's skill as a musician was plain to all. Before the evening was over, he was attempting Irish jigs, Italian boat songs, anything that they could sing, he would soon pick up on the violin, what the wharf people called Robbie's fiddle. After that, whenever the fishing vessels were in it was a time of music along the waterfront. Often they would join him with squeeze boxes or juice harps or whatever they had, filling the air with melodious sounds. Songs of joy and songs of sadness, songs of home and families left far across the sea.

The first week of September, Robbie and Elizabeth returned to school. Robbie would have been unhappy about not being able to help Brownie on the trawler, but he and Elizabeth had made new friends and would be joining them in the new school. The school was close–by and they could safely walk in the company of their many friends.

It was Saturday afternoon and Flo, Niki, Jenny, and the girls were taking a leisurely walk along the pier. Jacqueline had carefully checked her pockets to make sure she had a good supply of bread–crumbs to feed the sea gals. No amount of explanation could convince the little girl that not all gulls were of the female gender. Brownie had laughingly scoffed at any attempts made to change her mind stating that if all ships were 'shes' why couldn't all Jacqueline's gulls be gals?

As they neared the house on their way back, Elizabeth recognized Benjamin sitting alone on the steps waiting for their return.

"Hi, Uncle Ben," she yelled running ahead to greet him with Jacqueline close behind.

Ben and Martha came often but it was never often
enough for the children. Especially, since he usually had a
small treat for them somewhere in his pocket.

He greeted each of them by producing from his pockets
small bags of candy tied with a ribbon.

"Martha didn't come with you?" asked Jenny with a surprised look.

"No, something important has come up and I need to
speak with you personally," he stated in a professional tone.

Jenny, caught the seriousness of his mood and desire to
speak with her alone, "We can walk along the wharf and talk,"
she suggested.

"Me come to," said Jacqueline.

"No, we are going to make gingerbread," Flo reminded
her, "come on I need your help."

"'ats wight," stated Jacqueline thinking of the fun she
would have, "all wight, Uncle Ben. Me'll make 'ou a giner—
mans."

"That will be real nice," he smiled at the little girl as he
and Jenny walked away toward the wharf.

They walked in silence for a few moments along the
wharf. Jenny watched as the small boats moored in the slips
rolled gently with the gentle current. Anglers were bent over
their lines on the deeper side waiting in patient anticipation of
what might soon reward them for their expertise efforts. Oh,
how she loved the sea, with the smell of fish and the fresh salty
air. Far out on the water she could see a slight mist of fog
beginning to rise. Ordinarily that observation would have been
cause for concern for Robbie and Brownie's safe return from
the sea, but today Benjamin's thoughtful mood was greatly
diverting her attention.

He reached out and took her hand. He had never done
that before. Jenny wasn't sure if she was comfortable with this
gesture and sensing her thoughts, he timidly released her hand.

"Jenny," he said looking at her intently, "I have much to
tell you."

"Yes," she replied forebodingly, "I feel that you do."

"Jenny," he continued, "from the letters you gave to me and from the sources in St. Louis, Missouri, we have all the proof we need. It is important that you understand who you really are."

Jenny moved away from Benjamin slowly and then with quickening strides moved out along one of the piers that was almost abandoned of its usual fishing boats in the early afternoon. With rapid steps, Benjamin followed her.

"Jenny, you have to be told! You must listen to me," he persisted speaking kindly but firmly.

"I know," she replied softly almost as if to herself.

"What?" he questioned not hearing her reply.

"I said, I know," she repeated in a normal voice.

"What do you know?" he questioned again.

"I know you are going to tell me who I am," she replied as she looked up at him searchingly.

"Do you know—who you really are?" he asked.

"Sometimes I think I do, but most of the time I feel like I live in a fog, like that out there on the water. When it rolls in it gradually blanks out everything, just like my memories fade and then completely disappear from my mind," revealed Jenny trying to understand.

"First of all, Paulette was not your mother," affirmed Benjamin.

"Who was she then?" questioned Jenny meekly.

"No one of importance, not really," he explained, "but your real family, they are here in Boston and they are very eager to meet you."

"They know about me?" she asked still bewildered by the rapid revelation of events.

"Yes, they know and they are very happy and anxious to see you as soon as possible," he answered.

Jenny put her hands to her face and bowing her head begin to sob quietly.

"Jenny, dear Jenny," said Benjamin not knowing what to do, but trying to comfort her and now wishing Martha had come with him.

"Your grandmother is Rosetta Gordon, and Alex Gordon is your uncle," he revealed nervously with diminished excitement. "They are anxiously awaiting for you to join them. They wanted to come with me but I persuaded them that it was best that I speak with you first. I know that this is quite a shock and I wanted to relieve you of any apprehensions you may have."

"When can I meet them?" asked Jenny trying to control her crying

"Now, whenever you are ready," he responded.

"I don't think I can, now—I am too frightened," she replied with a trembling voice. "Where are they?" she asked looking straight ahead as if in thought.

"Waiting for you. Shall we go?" he asked while reaching for her hand.

Jenny slipped her hand into his and they walked to the house where Benjamin explained the situation to Niki and Flo.

As they traveled across town, Benjamin explained a great deal, filling in details along the way. Jenny sat still, like a frightened child, only asking a question now and then.

Chapter Twenty-One

The wind rustled with a placid whisper through the pine trees lining the short drive to the house. Jenny had been still most of the way, oblivious of what Ben had told Niki and Flo and not noticing their startled expressions. Now, as they approached the house she felt an unexplained attraction. Set back a distance from the street, it was very large and majestic, still there was an aura of warmth and unpretentious intimacy that seemed to reach out to her as she stared at it incredulously.

Ivy covered most of the brick on the lower floor and spiraled out onto a white arched trellis still covered with late blooming roses. It lent itself to a sense of disrepair and yet Jenny could see several men working in the garden just beyond the path that led through the trellised patio area.

Benjamin helped Jenny down from the carriage while she still kept her eyes focused on the house. He rang the bell and a servant appeared and gestured for them to enter and follow him to the broad hallway where an immense open stairway led elegantly to the upper floors. On the left was a spacious formal dining room and straight ahead down the hallway, Jenny was sure was a bright and cheery kitchen. To the right was a parlor and it was to this room where they were ushered.

"I have been here before, haven't I?" spoke Jenny with a guarded sense of certainty as she surveyed the room and every object that came into view. She crossed the room to the large bay windows and stared out across the well–kept lawns. It was bordered with shrubs and trees with stately homes on either side. Across the street were more imposing homes nestled within beautifully landscaped yards.

"Can it be that I am home?" she whispered as she became immersed in a feeling of sustained tranquility.

"Jenny," whispered Benjamin taking her by the arm as he stood behind her, "I would like to introduce you to your grandmother."

As Jenny slowly turned toward the sound of Benjamin's voice Rosetta held out her arms to the perplexed young lady. Slowly, Jenny submitted to her outstretched arms and moved into her warm embrace.

"Jenna, oh, Jenna—is it really you?" cried Rosetta as she embraced her and then with tear stained eyes held the young woman back a little to look searchingly into her face.

"Do you have any remembrance of me at all?" Rosetta questioned as tears continued to flow unashamedly down her cheeks.

"You, you came into the bakery one day, didn't you?" stated Jenny as she suddenly recognized Rosetta as the lady who had come into her shop and acted in such an unusual manner.

"Yes, yes, I did visit your shop," admitted Rosetta, "I had to see you for myself," she continued.

"The day you came, I felt like I knew you, but I just didn't know from where," related Jenny—her mouth dry and still uneasy about the sudden turn of events.

She felt a sudden touch on her arm and as Rosetta released her, Alex Gordon clutched her to him and cried with long aching sobs of relief and joy. Finally, he took her chin in his hand and lifted her face toward his.

"Do you remember me, Jenna?" he beseeched her.

Jenny looked long into his eyes.

"Yes," she murmured as a spark of recognition flickered from her subconscious into a full revelation, "Uncle Lixie, I think."

There were no dry eyes in the room or in the house for that matter. Word had spread throughout the house of Jenna's return and the servants were crowding the hallway for a glimpse of the long lost heiress. Rosetta, usually so in control, made no attempt to contain her emotions. She laughed and cried at the same time. Her cherished granddaughter was returned alive after all these years.

"May we call you Jenna?" she asked lovingly.

"Jenna? Jenna, is that truly my name?" asked Jenny as she remembered the surge of joy the discovery of that name had brought to her broken heart in the dim light on that far away farm.

With great certainty, Rosetta assured her that it was her name. In that hallowed moment, Jenny emerged from the darkness of her secluded cocoon and was set free like a butterfly just released. Oh the ecstasy, crescendoing throughout every fiber of her being. It was as if the light of this truth was reverberating throughout her palace.

Jenny was Jenna!

The dark webbed cocoon was as much a part of her as this moment of exhilarating beauty and release she now felt, but it could never again hold her enclosed within its restraining walls. No! Jenna was set free...forever free. She now knew unequivocally who she was.

"I am Jenna," she whispered. Then as this statement produced a more profound awareness of what it implied continued, "I am Jenna Gordon! I am Jenna Alexandria Gordon," she proclaimed aloud with astonishing authority.

Just then, she noticed that Martha had arrived and was weeping softly as she stood beside Alex. She was glad she had come and was happy she could share this moment with her.

However, sensing that there were important pieces of the puzzle missing she searched the room looking in vain for that special someone. That one whose image she carried in that locket. The one who was now revealed to her as her mother. Where was she? More than anyone else she longed to see her again face to face—no longer a veil of mystery between them—the woman in the locket was her mother but was conspicuously absent. Why? No one even mentioned her name or that of her father. Where were they? Her mind was racing now, grasping for answers to her questions. In the distant recesses of her mind, she could faintly hear Rosetta saying something, but she was now too shaken to hear. The ultimate realization of their probable death held her transfixed oblivious of anyone or anything else.

Jenna placed her hands over her eyes visibly shaken and began sobbing in disbelief. That haunting picture in the locket had brought her half way across the country in search of her.

Oh, how she wished she could have seen her once again. The grief was becoming too much to bear.

Suddenly, Jenna became startled by a commotion in the room, the soft approaching footsteps. Sensing something, she knew not what she slowly lowered her hands form her face and through a dewy veil faintly saw the beautiful figure of a lady. Wiping the tears from her eyes, she saw for the first time the lovely object of her quest—the lady from the locket. Trembling with a delicate feeling of joy, she became enraptured by the vision before her. Her hair was silken russet, graced with white about the temples. The face was more beautiful than the picture revealed or could have ever imagined. She smiled at Jenna, disclosing the delicate lines of maturity. Her eyes were as green as the Emerald Isles she came from and her expression was one of complete love and gratefulness as she now looked upon her only child who had risen from the grave. Carrie's eyes filled with tears and overflowed down her ivory cheeks, noticeably holding back the flood as she relished the moment, fastening her eyes upon her sweet precious Jenna.

"Mama, Oh, Mama," cried Jenna as they collapsed into each others arms shedding tears of joy and tears of remorse for all the years that had been stolen from them.

After a time, and no one really cared how long it was, Carrie took Jenna by the hand and ushered her toward the other side of the room by the open doorway.

"Jenna, dear, I want you to meet someone else," she said softly as Jenna with a weak smile lighting her now radiant face followed her obediently.

As Benjamin moved forward with a frail man in a wheelchair, Carrie pulled Jenna forward to meet her father, James, Jr.

"Jenna, this is your father."

The dear man was completely overcome with weeping, as was Jenna and everyone else in the room, and no one tried to hold back their tears of joy. It was a reunion that would never be forgotten in the Gordon family and would be remembered with great tenderness and pride as it was rehearsed from generation to generation for many years to come.

Rosetta Gordon had carried a great burden herself. She had always known that Carrie and James, Jr. were alive. It was Carrie who had wished to become anonymous, the shipwreck creating a perfect alibi. James was so critically injured, that all was taken care of long before he was well enough to object. Rosetta visited them secretly many times, but carried out their wishes to conceal the fact that they had not perished when the ship sank. Rosetta took care of all their finances, including household expenses and medical bills. She secretly corresponded with them regularly, pleading with Carrie to please forgive Alex, as he had been fully crushed by the whole ordeal.

Finally, after many years of seclusion, Carrie began to attend a small village parish in the tiny Irish countryside where they made their home. She began to listen with rapt attention as the cleric taught from God's word. Her heart was opened to Jeremiah 29:13, "And ye shall seek me and find me, when ye shall search for me with all your heart." Carrie had sought long for some sustaining influence to regain meaning to life and she now found the one friend who understood the great need of her heart 'forgiveness', and as Christ forgave her so she now freely forgave Alex. Oh, how she wanted to tell him at that moment of release from the heavy burden of her heart, but she was afraid. Finally, the wire came from Rosetta urging her and James to return home.

Rosetta had so wanted to make things right and the night of the ball she determined to bring James and Carrie home. Immediately after sending the cablegram, she began to restore to its former grandeur the house that they had left unattended for so many years.

Rosetta had put her life on the line, so to speak, and with great mental anguish had attempted to explain everything to Alex. Surprisingly he had taken it far better than she had expected. In fact as the days passed it became very evident that the news had elevated his spirit to a plateau of expectancy and joy. He eagerly with great anticipation with unabated joy and happiness waited for Carrie and James to arrive home.

That first meeting, when their eyes met, Carrie and Alex hesitant at first, then simultaneously embraced each other lovingly. There was no need for words of why or what or for any words of forgiveness, they both felt within their own hearts complete deliverance form all and any constraining oppressive influences that had come between them so many years ago.

Jenna looked up from where she had been kneeling by the wheelchair of her father as Niki, Brownie, and Flo entered the room with the children. Carrie knelt beside James and with open arms welcomed the children, explaining to them that she was their grandmother. James, his eyes showing what he could not speak, his expressions of joy, also extended his arms to greet them warmly. It was evident that there was a bond of kinship between them shared by each one, a bond of a loving personal attachment.

Throughout the many hours of that evening, extending into the early hours of the next morning they shared with each other their joy and news about the events of the intervening years. They were too overjoyed to notice the time or care about sleeping, but at the break of dawn the need for sleep overtook them one by one and as they each retired, they went to sleep with the joyous and reassuring realization of a new beginning.

Chapter Twenty–Two

Spring had come and again ambitious gardeners were hard at work endeavoring to restore the once lovely garden to its original state. Workmen were putting the finishing touches to the many repairs that had been needed upon the once resplendent green house.

James, Jr., Jenna's father, had left the confines of his wheelchair and once again turned his affection toward the task of growing his prize–winning orchids. While he busied himself utilizing his special skills with loving care he nevertheless enthusiastically looked forward to the soon probability of again rejoining Alex, his brother, in the family business. For a man whose life had seemed over, it was a true miracle. James could hardly speak when he and Carrie had returned to Boston, and was dependent on others to help him to and from the wheelchair to which he was confined. However, shortly after Jenna's homecoming, while James was seated in the garden watching the children at play, his power of speech returned to him. Not long after that, he began taking steps as Jenna and Carrie held his arms and walked with him along the garden paths. Before the first snows of winter had fallen, James could walk without any assistance.

Carrie was ecstatic in her happiness. Her life was enriched with riches far beyond the mundane—far beyond the affluent life of luxury. All that was associated with family, friends, love, joy and peace. Her loving husband, James, was almost completely well, and Jenna, her precious child, though now a grown woman, had been graciously returned to her. True, the lost years of separation could not be returned but she and her daughter gleaned the most from every precious moment spent together. Then there were the dear children. Oh, how she adored them. Such an added blessing they were to her life. Truly, she felt that her 'cup runneth over'.

The house that had been home to Jenna for six short years before her abduction was now once again filled to near capacity with happy family members. James and Carrie had abandoned it—their grief over Jenna's disappearance so unbearable that they lost interest in staying there and the will to continue their lives in such a familiar but now dismal setting. But, now the house was alive again with joyful family members and cheerful friends.

James and Carrie settled in a large guest bedroom with its own sitting room on the main floor of the house. When Jenna returned James could not manage to climb stairs, but now was well able to maneuver them with ease. It was their idea that Jenna should occupy their original room with adjoining nursery on the second floor. Jacqueline was completely satisfied with the old nursery restored exactly as Jenna, her mother, had left it and prepared to claim it as her own. She promised to tenderly care for the long forgotten toys and promptly set about extending to them her child–like mothers love. Many hours were spent with Jenna and Jacqueline together in that room being joined often by Carrie and Elizabeth and sometimes even, Robbie.

Elizabeth and Robbie had rooms across the hall from Jenna's. Although the house had been restored with great care in every detail to the best of Rosetta's judgment, Elizabeth's room was not suitably decorated for a little girl. The room had ample windows and good lighting but the walls were a somber gray and the furnishings too ornate and cumbersome—a setting not conducive to creating a cheerful atmosphere.

"How would you like your room decorated, Elizabeth?" asked Grandmother Carrie with warm enthusiasm while declaring the room totally unsuitable for her granddaughter.

"I would like it all in pink with rosebud wallpaper," she decided, giving much adult–like thought to the project.

It was settled, Grandmother Carrie had the room done exactly as Elizabeth desired. In the meantime, she gathered the children together for a trip to one of the finest establishments in Boston, where they each selected furniture, rugs, wallpaper, and curtains to their liking.

Soon, Elizabeth's room glowed with newly decorated walls of pink rosebud wallpaper with pink rugs covering the floor while organdy curtains, adorned with tiny rosebuds floating on a white background, hung at the windows and framed the white canopy bed.

Robbie was at first indifferent about the choice of color for the walls of his room and cared little about what material the curtains were made of, but he did find a bed that caught his interest. It was a replica of a captain's bunk from a ship. Grandma Carrie soon had his room transfixed into a reproduction of a captain's stateroom, complete with an authentic helm and sextant. Robbie was completely enchanted with it and chartered many an imaginary voyage with his friends using the chartered courses on the maps adorning the walls.

Alex had experienced the complete restoration of his life. Jenna and he became inseparable by an unbreakable bond of love and mutual understanding. Years of separation could not destroy their esteem for one another. Alex had also found perfect peace initiated by Carrie's forgiveness again viewing life with newly found vigor and vitality. His innate contagious personality and happy disposition returned, however, never again would he indulge himself in the baser things of life. Instead, this gifted and talented individual became a new creature in Christ under the astute guidance of Jenna and Carrie.

Grandmother Rosetta, grand in every way once again, became the adoring grandmother she had been to Jenna long ago. With great ceremony, she restored to Robbie, Elizabeth, and Jacqueline all that had been lost to Jenna. The children brought endless delight to everyone.

Uncle Lixie, as the children soon nicknamed Alex, and grandmother Rosetta's grand mansion was only a short distance away and rooms which were once uninviting and coldly silent were now alive with joyous shouts of laughter as the three children regularly visited them. Their many friends became familiar faces in a widening circle of friendships, some becoming more close and intimate as they grew up together into adulthood and later life.

Rosetta lived to be nearly one–hundred years old, continuing to be a constant influence and source of strength and integrity to the entire family who she do dearly loved and watched over with tender affection mixed with proper austerity.

Robbie's lung condition seemed to leave him weak at times but the best of care, love, and attention resulted in a generally healthy and abundantly happy young man. His fascination and devotion for the violin continually increased as with excellent training he began to receive recognition throughout the Boston area as a violin virtuoso expanding later to a national and then international scope. Also, Grandfather James and Uncle Lixie with pride introduced Robbie to the grand business of shipbuilding.

Elisabeth continued to be a devoted sister to Robbie while committing herself to the piano. She was not especially enraptured with it, but did enjoy music and most certainly had a unique talent in fact, had she any real regard for her own capabilities she would undoubtedly have become well know as a pianist herself. Instead, she much preferred to remain anonymous as Robbie's accompanist and share the acclaim he received. Her keen sense of humor and her amusing antics made her a popular choice with everyone. She and Jacqueline both became Boston's most beautiful and sought after socialites.

Jacqueline was sweet and adoring, proper in every way and had the distinctive ability to express her love for each member of the family and friends without reservation. Far different from her humble beginnings on the remote farm in Kansas, she now grew up in a life of affluence, love, and stability. Her stunning beauty and effervescent but generous nature were unsurpassed.

Jenna never forgot her dear friends who had helped her and worked so faithfully at her side through trying and difficult times. She persuaded Alex to promote Brownie to an important position at the Gordon Shipbuilding Company, which because of his vast knowledge of ships, proved to be a most rewarding mutual arrangement. He became an integral part in the development of great steamships, which he greatly admired and had an affinity for.

Niki and Brownie purchased a fine house close to Jenna's and they continued to remain very close friends throughout the years.

Flo Ashten remained with the family, by choice, having become an inherent part of the family. In fact, everyone naturally accepted her as a blood–relative, one who became as an indispensable part of the family. She had her own room not wanting to live in a house alone, and an ample allotment and was free to do as she pleased, but chose to spend her time with the family and especially with the children. The bond between them was strong and the children grew up thinking of her as an aunt or perhaps a cousin, but to them she was ever and always just Flo. She was always there, a warm caring friend in whom they could confide or present a pressing problem, or whatever the need may be, she was there for them.

Chapter Twenty – Three

Today was an extremely exciting day for the Gordons. The late spring garden at the Gordon Mansion was groomed to perfection. Huge baskets and vases of flowers were everywhere complimenting the flawlessly kept grounds adorned with its many sculptured shrubs and beautifully arranged flower–beds. The fruit trees in full blossom dotted about the landscape permeating the air with its floral essence. This grand display and profusion of colors provided a picturesque setting for what was about to take place.

Servants, in their finest uniforms hurried about meticulously taking care of last minute details. Each one performing their individual tasks with efficient endeavor.

In the still, hushed presence of an overflowing congregation Jenna walked slowly down the long aisle. The church was resplendent with its intricate patterns of opulent gold and medieval tones of wood and stone beautified by the rays of the sun streaming through subdued hues of stained glass windows depicting sacred Biblical scenes. Strains of wedding music softly flowed from the organ and filled the sanctuary.

Benjamin stood waiting at the altar. He nervously smiled to her as she neared the front. Jenna stepped forward and took her place.

The words of the ceremony were spoken with tenderness and devotion as each of the rapturous couple vowed they would share their lives together from that day forward with God as their witness.

Benjamin looked down adoringly at Jenna as she took his arm and they joined the wedding party in the receiving line.

"Oh, Martha, you are such a beautiful bride!" exclaimed one guest after another as they greeted the happy couple and the wedding party.

Alex, handsome and beaming with love, had eyes only for his radiant bride, Martha, who clung fast to his arm.

"How strange and wonderful is the path of life," thought Jenna as she looked with great affection upon her dear family and devoted friends. Throughout the coming years she would encounter joyful times and sad, she would be mother and daughter and friend, but she would live her life now, as the person she was born to be, and but for a few guided steps may never have come to know.

What Satan meant for evil, God has turned for good. Yes, 'weeping may endure for a night, but joy cometh in the morning.'

Printed in the United States
4628